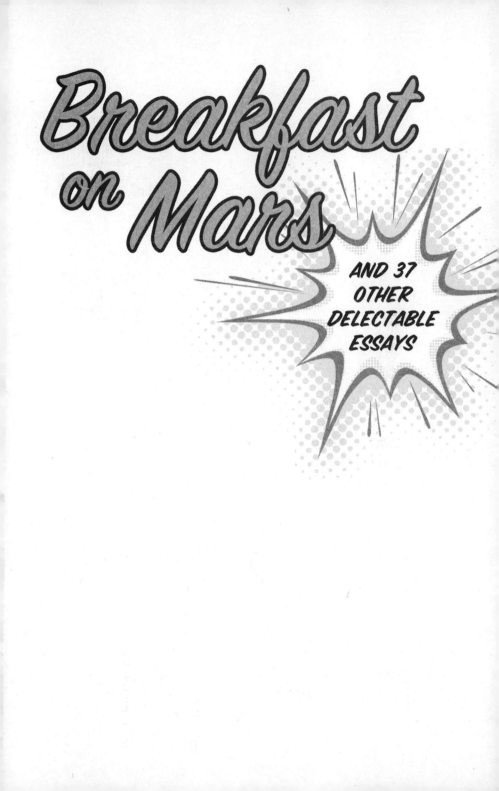

Breakfast on Mars

AND 37 OTHER DELECTABLE ESSAYS

Breakfast on Mars

AND 37 OTHER DELECTABLE ESSAYS

Edited by **REBECCA STERN** & **BRAD WOLFE**

ROARING BROOK PRESS New York

Published by Roaring Brook Press
Roaring Brook Press is a division of Holtzbrinck Publishing Holdings Limited Partnership
175 Fifth Avenue, New York, New York 10010
mackids.com
All rights reserved

Library of Congress Cataloging-in-Publication Data

Breakfast on Mars and 37 Other Delectable Essays / Edited by Rebecca Stern and Brad Wolfe.
    pages cm
    ISBN 978-1-59643-737-1 (hardcover)—ISBN 978-1-59643-881-1 (ebook)
    1. English language—Composition and exercises—Study and teaching (Elementary)   2. English language—Composition and exercises—Study and teaching (Middle school)   3. Essay—Authorship.
I. Stern, Rebecca.   II. Title: Breakfast on Mars and thirty-seven Other Delectable Essays.
    LB1576.B5967 2013
    372.62'3—dc23

                                                                                2012040918

The editors are donating a portion of the proceeds from this collection to Free the Children, an education-focused charity organization that inspires young people to develop as socially conscious global citizens through domestic empowerment programs, leadership training, and international development programs. Interested readers may find more information at freethechildren.com

Roaring Brook Press books may be purchased for business or promotional use.
For information on bulk purchases please contact Macmillan Corporate and Premium Sales Department at (800) 221-7945 x5442 or by email at specialmarkets@macmillan.com.

First edition 2013
Printed in the United States of America by RR Donnelley & Sons Company, Harrisonburg, Virginia

10 9 8 7 6 5 4 3 2 1

For the essay writers of the universe—past, present, and future.

—*B. S. & B. W.*

STARTERS

ENTREES

DESSERT

Foreword

I have always been a voracious and eclectic reader. Once my eyes began to form an understanding of letters, then words, then sentences, then paragraphs—I was hooked. I read and read and was offered books by teachers and librarians, which I would pretend to read, but really I would hide forbidden tomes inside them—like collections of Dear Abby columns and various articles about household hints and other obscure topics that no other ten-year-old would ever be interested in.

I first learned of my writing ability when I was about ten, when my class got in trouble for unruliness as a group and our punishment was to write essays about what we had done. This I take a major issue with—Teachers, do not use writing as punishment. It's damaging and crippling and ruthless and cruel. Do not make kids write sentences over and over, and do not make them write about things they truly do not care about as you will make them hate writing.

Writing is an art and a gift and a privilege and a lifesaver, and if children learn that it is meant to be torture they will never discover that. They will forever associate writing with cramped hands and blurry vision, and there will be a generation of writers whose writing could have saved the world that will never come to be because you couldn't think of anything better to keep them in line.

Because of writing sentences as punishment, I hold pencils incorrectly. I lay them in between my second and third fingers rather than gripping them between my thumb and index finger.

Thankfully my father let me use his typewriter or I would never have blossomed as a writer like I eventually did. The essay that made me realize I was a writer was handwritten. It was a scathing criticism of the teacher and the values held by the school. It was personal and it was nasty and it was sarcastic, and I wish that I could print here what was written there, but the essay was handed in and then sent directly to the principal's office along with yours truly some hours later.

The principal, a Nervous Nellie of a woman, breathed hard as she read my essay aloud back to me. She read passages, which I cannot remember now (I wish I did) and then said, "I must admit this is good writing, but . . ." and then proceeded to try to punish me verbally, but not having really anything to say except compliments, she couldn't really go anywhere with the insults. She knew I was smart and she couldn't punish me for it. She knew what I had produced was satire, but she didn't understand it and she didn't know what to do with it and so she just kind of sputtered out. I left the principal's office and wandered in the weird dead space between the classrooms and the teachers' lounge. I took the long way back because I treasured the silence of the hallways and the kids all in their desks and me free to roam without even a heavy wooden hall pass or a need to go to the bathroom.

Later, I stood by the teachers' lounge where an intense cluster of polyester-clad men and women who were younger than I am now sat together and gossiped in hushed voices. I listened as they read my essay aloud to each other. I heard my words bandied about and there were accusations of plagiarism, but that was argued because the insults were too specific, too spot-on—where could I have copied them? They laughed at my jokes and my astute, tight-as-a-drum writing, and they agreed that I should be punished, but they were at a loss trying to figure out how.

I believe I paid for my indulgence with a call to my parents—who didn't really seem to care because they were just too tired from working day and night—and some after-school detentions, which consisted of me sitting in an empty classroom with a physical education teacher, silently doing my homework until the sky grew dark.

In the end, I felt like I won something. I realized that my words had power. The way I put them together had a charge and an electricity and an energy that I could use to hurt and maim, but also to praise and worship. I discovered the pleasure of committing ideas to paper and that the things in my head had little trouble on their way through my heart and into my hands. I was a writer then, and I am one now. And I am good.

This anthology that you're about to read is what I wish I had growing up—a collection of essays by authors who also realize the power of words, who understand that writing about ideas should be fun and real, not a drill. The authors in this book get that essays don't have to follow the same rules that someone made up forever ago. They believe that boundaries can be crossed and lines erased, and that sometimes the weirdest ideas are the best ones. I wish my teachers had handed me this collection and asked me to write about things I was interested in, things I cared about. I wish my teachers could have shown me that real writers write essays too and not just kids who are in trouble. Here's what you should know—your words have meaning; they have just as much power as mine or as anyone else's. Step outside the lines. Your words can save the world.

Margaret Cho

A Special Note to Teachers

"If you want to be a writer," Stephen King accurately prescribes in *On Writing*, "you must do two things above all others: read a lot and write a lot." As teachers, we put this principle into effect when we teach kids the craft of fiction writing and poetry. Yet, when it comes to teaching kids how to write essays, King's advice is discarded. We let kids plow ahead into this genre without arming them with inspiring examples. In a way, it's like handing someone an address without giving him directions. We need a map to know where we're going. We need to visualize what's ahead. Great essays are the maps our kids need.

The challenge we face in inspiring our students in the essay genre is a difficult one. There is simply a big difference between the availability of young adult fiction and poetry on the one hand, and essays on the other. As Lucy Calkins writes in her nationally used teaching manual, *Breathing Life into Essays* (Heinemann, 2006):

One of the challenges in this unit of study is that I don't have published examples of essays that resemble those I'll ask children to write. The essays by authors like E. B. White and John McPhee are far more complex than those that children can write, and children's bookshelves don't contain anthologies of essays written specifically for youngsters.

In addition, go-to online teaching tools are forced to recommend suboptimal solutions, even going so far as to encourage teachers to write their own essays as examples. Imagine writing a novel just to show your kids what a real novel looked like! Preposterous.

We know that teachers spend hours searching for age-appropriate, well-written essays to use in the classroom. (Believe us, we've been there!) And so, we put together *this collection* to fill that void and to make it easier for you. We—along with all of the incredible authors in this book—want students to see that essays can be just as enjoyable to read as fiction (perhaps even more so!). Furthermore, we want our students to recognize that essays have a place in the "real world" and not just in classrooms. Real authors write real essays. Authors that they may already know and love think essays are cool. Let's help inspire kids toward a deeper joy of writing, words, communication, and ideas. Let's give them essays they'll actually love.

Rebecca and Brad

Introduction

You're going to write an essay about what? Eating breakfast on Mars? Bathing with spiders? Why humans need tails? That's preposterous! Essays are supposed to be serious and structured, right?

WRONG!

For too long, we have held essays captive in the world's most boring zoo. We've taken all the wild words, elaborate arguments, and big hairy ideas found in essays, and we've poached them from their natural habitat. We've locked essays in an artificial home.

Fiction? You can roam free! Say whatever you want, however you want. Poetry, you get to dance and sing. Art, do back flips and cartwheels, for all we care!

But, Essay, we must tame you. We must squish you into five paragraphs, and we must give you so much structure that you cower in the corner, scared for your life.

The essay's fate has long looked bleak. But do not despair,

for change is brewing. In the following pages, you'll catch a glimpse of something most people have never seen in the wild. We've let essays out of their cages, and we've set them loose. We've allowed them to go back to their roots.

After all, essays weren't always tame. It was in the 1500s that a Frenchman named Montaigne first wrote exploratory nonfiction pieces—some serious, some playful, some short, some long—in which he experimented with writing about things that mattered to him. He called his form of expression *essais*—which, in English, means "trials" or "attempts." (Notice, *essay* doesn't stem from a root that means "to cage" or "to bore.")

Montaigne rocked the world with this new genre. His writing showed people that it was cool to try to figure out answers to crazy questions, to think deeply, and to expound on wild ideas. After his first collection was published and praised, people started to emulate his style and form. People started to write their own trials and attempts.

Essays were once hip. They were once provocative. But then came the Dark Age of the Essay. Sometime in the 1800s, essays were rounded up and captured, and they inevitably started losing their flair. As mechanization spread, schools began teaching essays in a similarly rigid way; creative, divergent essays became nearly extinct as each one was encouraged to be the same as the last. Before long, schools were filled to the brim with tired, unlively essays. And sadly, not much has changed since.

Breakfast on Mars features thirty-seven amazing authors who have returned essays to the wild. Through taking on the most fun, challenging essay assignments out there and crafting original essays of all types—persuasive, literary, personal, informative, and even graphic—these authors show us that essays don't have to be any one particular way. In fact, when essays are allowed to be themselves, they can be every which way. They can be anything. They can laugh and breathe and cry and dream. They can send dogs to the moon, put tails on humans, wear invisibility cloaks, and bathe with spiders. Essays can do a lot when offered the chance. When given back their freedom, essays are truly something to behold.

PERSONAL ESSAY

Describe a time you had to do something you really didn't want to do.

Camp Dread or How to Survive a Shockingly Awful Summer

by RANSOM RIGGS

It took me about a week to realize I'd been suckered. The ad in the church bulletin had called it a "horseback riding" camp, but by the end of week one, the only thing I'd learned about horses was how to scrape their stalls clean, and the only thing I'd ridden was an electric fence, which I had backed into in what was probably a subconscious escape attempt. But there was no escaping. I was stuck in the swampy middle of nowhere. Cell phones hadn't been invented yet, and neither I nor the other campers had the guts to complain to the swaggering, dip-spitting cowboys who served as both our camp counselors and de facto prison guards. As that fence launched me into the air, arms flailing like a rodeo clown, butt tingling with residual electricity, I made a solemn pledge to myself: *never again.*

I ended up at horse camp because my mother had decided it was important for me to try new things—her definition of which apparently did not extend to watching new movies at the multiplex or playing new Nintendo 64 games in various friends' basements, which had previously comprised my entire plan for the summer. She had never objected to my lazy summers before, and after nine months of the exceptional torment that was sixth grade, I thought I deserved one more than ever. So naturally I felt a little betrayed when, a mere week after school had ended, she announced that I was off to camp in a few days. And not just any camp—*horse* camp.

I was baffled too and Mom was short on answers to my many questions. Was I being punished for something? What imaginary crime had I supposedly committed? Did she think I'd actually have *fun*? I couldn't imagine why, as I'd never expressed even the slightest interest in horses, or horse-related camps, or camps in general. Then, after remembering how the few girls' rooms I'd seen the inside of had been veritable shrines to horses, an admittedly unlikely explanation occurred to me: *My mother thinks I'm a girl.*

I tried explaining to her that I wasn't a girl, that I didn't know the first thing about horses and didn't care to, and that living in an un-air-conditioned cabin with strangers in the sweltering summer heat of Central Florida made little sense when I had air-conditioning and video games and friends to play them with at home. She acted as if she hadn't heard me.

When arguing failed, I tried begging. When begging had no effect, I resorted to silent fuming and passive-aggressive door slamming. Despite everything, she would not be swayed.

"It's only camp," she said. "You'll survive."

Finally, all that was left for me to do was dread.

There were so many things to dread about this camp that it was hard to know which to focus on. There was the inescapable heat, the nightly hymn-singing—an inevitable feature of church-affiliated camps—and the possibility of being kicked at, gnawed on, thrown from, or otherwise molested by a horse. But the pit-of-my-stomach dread, the thing I went to bed dreading and woke up in the morning still dreading, was that for the first time in as long as I could remember, I would be stuck in a place where I had absolutely no friends. Hymns and horse tramplings are survivable provided you have a friend to share your misery with, but I would be leaving my merry band of like-minded nerds behind, and had no idea how to replace them on short notice.

The popular kids I knew seemed to make friends effortlessly. Their cliques grew and blossomed and rotated members on a daily basis. My friend group, on the other hand, was like a rare mold that only grew beneath a certain kind of rock at a specific elevation: There wasn't much of it, it formed very slowly, and it was exceedingly stable. But if a wild mongoose came and ate a bunch of it, the mold wasn't going to grow back in any big hurry. In other words, I knew how to *have* friends, but I'd had them for so long I couldn't remember how to *make* them—and I wasn't at all certain I could learn.

The fateful day arrived. I tossed a bag of wrinkled clothes into the trunk of my mom's car and slumped into the passenger seat. We left our beach-adjacent suburb for the mosquito-haunted swamps of Florida's primeval interior. The farther inland we drove, the wilder the landscape became. First, the chain stores and strip malls faded away. Then the road narrowed from four lanes to two, towered over by giant, grasping live oaks hung with nets of swaying Spanish moss. Long stretches of pavement had no markings at all save the polka-dot speckle of squashed armadillos. Along the shoulder, deep ditches brimmed with drowning pools of stagnant rainwater.

"You'll have a nice time," Mom said. "You'll see."

I felt like I was being driven to my own funeral.

After what seemed like hours, we finally arrived at the camp: a cluster of squat cabins, a stable, a few dusty campsites. We pulled into a parking lot crowded with mud-splashed pickup trucks and got out, and that's when I caught my first glimpse of the kids who would be my fellow campers. They were all milling around the campsite, acting bored and cool, every one of them wearing variations of the same outfit: cowboy boots, T-shirt tucked into high-waisted jeans, baseball cap with the bill curled into a little tunnel that hid the eyes from view. As I stood watching them, country music whining from a stereo somewhere, I realized that the main problem with horse camp wouldn't be the lack of air-conditioning or the bugs or being forced to interact with large animals that presumably wanted nothing to do with me, but that horse camp would be populated with the sort of kids who *wanted* to be at horse camp, who *liked* the idea of spending weeks in the hot middle of nowhere pretending to be cowboys. Among people like that, I may as well have been an alien.

In that instant, I gave up all hope of making friends and resigned myself to being a loner for the next two weeks. Now I know what you're probably thinking—and you're wrong. This isn't one of those stories where the popular kid defends me from a bully and we become besties for life and the reader learns a valuable lesson about how much rednecks from the boonies and nerds from the suburbs have in common. I'd made up my mind that horse camp was going to be the worst two weeks ever, and that's more or less what it was. I barely talked to anyone. I shoveled a lot of horse poop. A kid they called Big Dan pushed me around a little, but my response to his taunts was so muted—I'd long ago learned not to give bullies what they wanted, which was a big reaction—that he quickly moved on to another target. Mostly I was just lonely and bored; the most exciting thing that happened was that I got a jaggedy-looking scar on my butt where I touched that electric fence.

Eventually camp ended, and my mom came to pick me up. She asked how it was and I said "horrible" and told her about my solemn pledge never to go to camp again, and she seemed okay with it. As far as she was concerned, I had experienced something new, and that had been the whole idea. That the new thing had been feeling like a giant unfriendable loser for two weeks was beside the point.

As for my pledge, it lasted exactly three years. I'd kind of gotten it into my head that I wanted to be a writer, and when I found out about this camp for young writers that met every summer at a college in Virginia, I decided against my better judgment to give it a try. This time, though, I convinced a friend from home to go with me, as a sort of insurance policy, in case the kids at writing camp were scary or weird or didn't like me. I didn't spend too much time worrying about it, though, and I think that made all the difference.

Neither of us had trouble making friends at writing camp, even though the kids there came from lots of different back-grounds and liked all kinds of different things. I had the time of my life, went back the next two summers, and now, years later, am proud to count some of the people I met there among my best friends.

So it turned out that I was totally friendable after all, and I'd been way overthinking the whole how-you-make-friends thing. I thought about it so much, in fact, that back in horse camp I'd gotten discouraged and given up on new-friend-making entirely. I had a terrible time because I told myself I would, and in the sixth grade, being right had been more im-portant to me than being happy. But for all my self-inflicted suffering, it was Mom who was right: It was only camp. I sur-vived.

I still don't like horses, though.

Ransom Riggs is the *New York Times* bestselling author of *Miss Peregrine's Home for Peculiar Children* and *Talking Pictures*. He lives in Los Angeles, where in his spare time he makes short films, collects old photos, and travels as much as he possibly can.

Sasquatch Is Out There
(And He Wants Us to Leave Him Alone)

by KIRSTEN MILLER

A species of large, apelike creatures inhabits the forests of America's Pacific Northwest. We call them Sasquatch or Bigfoot. Although we do not know what they call themselves, they almost certainly have a name for their kind. The Sasquatch are hairy, but that doesn't mean that they're unintelligent. The fact that we still haven't proved that the Sasquatch exist suggests that the species may be smarter than we ever imagined.

There is ample evidence that we share this continent with an unidentified species. Anthropologists say Native Americans were telling tales of giant, "hairy men" long before outsiders ever arrived on these shores.[1] These days, the enormous footprints that gave Bigfoot his name are frequently discovered by hikers and hunters. Many of the prints may be hoaxes, but experts insist that a few are so detailed that they couldn't be fake.[2]

---

1 David J. Daegling, *Bigfoot Exposed: An Anthropologist Examines America's Enduring Legend* (AltaMira Press, 2004).

2 Jeffrey Meldrum, *Sasquatch: Legend Meets Science* (Macmillan, 2007).

Swatches of coarse, reddish hair have been collected near Sasquatch tracks and sightings. According to Dr. Jeffrey Meldrum, associate professor of anatomy and anthropology at Idaho State University, some of these samples appear to belong to a species of primate. But the hair isn't human—and it doesn't match any other ape in the database. Whatever the mysterious creatures may be, thousands of eyewitnesses—including police officers and pastors—have reported encounters with them. Hundreds of people have even managed to catch a Sasquatch on camera. Unfortunately, the pictures tend to be grainy, and the videos are often out of focus. The Sasquatch almost always refuse to pose.

Yet despite all the evidence, many (okay, *most*) scientists claim that the Sasquatch are nothing more than a legend. They all hang their hats on one simple fact: We've been searching for years, but we've never produced a body. A living Sasquatch has never been captured. The remains of dead specimens have never been found.

Even the rarest, most elusive creatures end up shot by hunters, captured by researchers, or flattened by speeding cars, the skeptics will say. No wild animal is crafty enough to avoid us forever. However, there may be a simple reason why the Sasquatch continue to give us the slip. Perhaps they aren't wild animals. We see photos of furry beasts and immediately assume they're no smarter than your average gorilla. But what if we've been underestimating the Sasquatch all these years? Perhaps they aren't beasts at all, but an unknown species of human.

Stick with me here, because this is not quite as crazy as it sounds. We (*Homo sapiens*) are not the only species of human to have called this planet home. In 1829, bones of another species, the Neanderthals (*Homo neanderthalensis*), were first discovered in Belgium. These big, brawny hominids once mingled with our kind in Europe and Asia.[3] While they are often portrayed as dimwitted brutes, Neanderthals were a fairly intelligent bunch. Not only were they as smart as our ancestors, it's possible that the two groups could have mated,[4] which means the Neanderthals may actually be ancestors to millions of you. (Please note that I didn't say *us*.)

For almost two hundred years after that big Belgian discovery, everyone was completely convinced that the *Homo* family tree had only two branches. Then in 2003, archaeologists uncovered proof that a tiny, hobbitlike species now known as Flores Man (*Homo floresiensis*) lived in the jungles of Indonesia as recently as twelve thousand years ago.[5] Evidence of a fourth human species, the Denisovans, was found in a Russian cave in 2010.[6]

Throughout the twentieth century, the scientific community would have laughed at anyone who had dared suggest that four species of humans might have once shared the earth. None of

3 *Human Evolution*. The Smithsonian Institution's Human Origins Program. Smithsonian Institute, humanorigins.si.edu/ (accessed February 2, 2012).

4 Paul Rincon, "Neanderthal Genes Survive in Us," *BBC News*, May 6, 2010. news.bbc.co.uk/2/hi/science/nature/8660940.stm (accessed February 2, 2012).

5 Robin McKie, "How a Hobbit Is Rewriting the History of the Human Race." *The Guardian*, February 21, 2010. www.guardian.co.uk/science/2010/feb/21/hobbit-rewriting-history-human-race (accessed February 2, 2012).

6 Nicholas Wade, "Bone May Reveal a New Human Group," *New York Times*, March 24, 2010, www.nytimes.com/2010/03/25/science/25human.html (accessed February 2, 2012).

those scientists are laughing right now. Today, most would admit that more unknown species could be awaiting discovery. Archaeologists all over the world are currently ransacking caves, searching for the bones of manlike creatures that have been extinct for thousands of years.

But if we know there have been other types of humans, why would we assume that *Homo sapiens* is the only group to survive to the present day? Perhaps there's another living species of human—a hairy distant cousin that looks as little like us as the burly Neanderthals or miniature Flores Man. Our scientists may be out digging for fossils, but the undiscovered species they're seeking could be hiding—and thriving—in our own backyards.

Is it possible that an intelligent hominid species could remain undiscovered well into the twenty-first century? We can look to our fellow *Homo sapiens* for the answer. Around the globe, small tribes of human beings continue to live in complete isolation. They are often referred to as "uncontacted peoples" because they've had no known contact with the outside world. Between 2004 and 2007, twenty-seven such tribes were discovered in the nation of Brazil alone.[7] That's twenty-seven separate groups of people who were hunting, gathering, and raising their families in the Amazon basin—and the rest of us had no clue they were out there.

Of course, it would be foolish to assume that all "uncontacted" tribes know as little about us as we do about them.

---

7 FUNAI (Fundação Nacional do Índio), January 18, 2007.

Some of the tribes may have been studying us for years. Perhaps we haven't "found" them because, like the Sasquatch, they don't want us to find them.

If you're part of a small tribe that doesn't want to be bothered, the Amazon jungle may be the perfect place to call home. But the Pacific Northwest isn't a bad bet, either. There are 4.6 million acres of protected forest on the American side.[8] Add in the woodlands of neighboring Canada, and you have more than enough wilderness to shelter and feed nomadic tribes of Sasquatch. From time to time, a few curious individuals may leave the dense forest to sneak a peek at the *Homo sapiens*, but the Sasquatch tribes have learned it's best to avoid people and their guns. The fact that they choose to steer clear of us—a species that decorates its homes with the heads of other animals—may be the most convincing proof that the Sasquatch possess high intelligence.

So if the Sasquatch are smart and do their best to avoid discovery, it's not surprising that we've never managed to capture a live specimen. Then bring us a corpse, the skeptics will say—as if the Sasquatch were unfeeling brutes who abandon their dead. Even if that were the case, a carcass wouldn't last long on the forest floor. But most intelligent species don't leave the bodies of their friends and family to be picked over by scavengers. Perhaps the Sasquatch bury their dead or dispose of the corpses in bodies of water. And there's always a chance that they eat their

---

8 USDA Forest Service.

deceased loved ones the way the Neanderthals did. (There's a very big difference between smart and civilized.)

In conclusion, it is entirely plausible that the Sasquatch aren't monsters, apes, or mythical creatures, but rather an unknown species of human. Highly intelligent hominids, they may live in small tribes that wander the vast North American wilderness. They care for their young and dispose of their dead. And they do not want the pleasure of our company.

Those who accept that the Sasquatch are out there—but find it hard to imagine that they might be intelligent—would be wise to keep one thing in mind. We, *Homo sapiens*, have a very long history of underestimating our fellow animals. (Did you know crows can count? That elephants paint and mourn their dead? That dolphins speak in their own private language? I've even seen a chicken play tic-tac-toe.) Let's be honest, if the Sasquatch were a little less hairy, they would probably get far more respect.

Of course, there will always be die-hard skeptics who will need to see a body before they concede that the Sasquatch are real. But there is one thing upon which everyone can agree: The world would be a much more interesting place if the Sasquatch did exist.

Kirsten Miller grew up in a small town in the mountains of North Carolina. At seventeen, she hit the road and moved to New York City, where she lives to this day. Kirsten is the author of the acclaimed Kiki Strike books, which tell the tale of the delinquent girl geniuses who keep Manhattan safe.

Warning: This Essay Does Not Contain Pictures

by SCOTT WESTERFELD

Cast your mind back. Remember when you were seven or eight years old and, for the first time, someone handed you a book with no pictures.

"No pictures?" you may have asked. "Well, this kind of sucks."

Sure, the pictures had been getting fewer and the print size smaller as you got older, but suddenly here was a book with zero pictures. The adult handing you the book had an explanation: "You're a big kid now, and big kids don't like pictures in their books. Now you get to use your imagination!"

Maybe you were suspicious of this argument at first. Yes, you were a big kid, but you had nothing against pictures. The images in your books had never stopped you from using your imagination before. As time passed, though, you got used to books having no pictures. Why would a novel for adults or teenagers need illustrations? Picture books are for little kids, right?

Well, I'm here to tell you something. Your suspicions back

then were correct; everything that helpful adult was telling you was a lie.

To understand how this lie got started, let's go back a hundred years. Most novels back then, whether for adults or children, were illustrated. Most of the classic novels you read in high school English class these days—*Pride and Prejudice, Vanity Fair, War of the Worlds*—used to have pictures in them. A century ago, it wasn't just little kids who liked images with their stories. Everyone did.

Back then, in fact, illustrators could be as well known as writers. Charles Dickens's first novel, *The Pickwick Papers*, wasn't published because someone wanted to read Dickens. It was commissioned as a text to accompany drawings by Robert Seymour. Seymour was the rock star; Dickens was a hanger-on. Illustrators were also important in the creation of characters. You know that funny hat Sherlock Holmes always wears? It's called a deerstalker cap and has become the symbol for Holmes and for literary detectives in general. But if you read the original Sherlock Holmes stories, you won't find the words *deerstalker cap* even once. It was Sidney Paget, the illustrator, who added the distinctive hat to the character, not writer Sir Arthur Conan Doyle.

So how did we get from a world where illustrations were plentiful, and where illustrators could be powerful partners in creation, to our modern-day world, where there are hardly any pictures in novels at all?

It's easy to forget that a century ago, everyone lived in a

hand-drawn world. When you opened up the sports pages back then, you'd find a drawing of yesterday's game. The products in mail-order catalogs were drawn, not photographed. And if your house burned down in the middle of the night and you were standing outside watching everything you owned go up in smoke, next to you would be an artist from the local paper— drawing your house burn down! Nobody thought this was weird at all.

In those days, every city needed artists to fill the newspapers with realistic art, to draw campaign posters, ads for toothpaste, catalog images, whatever. This army of illustrators made it easy for publishing companies to add pictures to their books. Not just stories for little kids, but novels for adults, as well. So they did, because people liked them.

But starting in the early twentieth century, that illustration industry began to disappear. Was it because adults no longer liked pictures? Because the world of readers had finally grown up? Because people's imaginations got better?

No, it was cameras.

Once cameras became cheap and plentiful, it was easier to send a photographer to the baseball game instead of an artist. Catalogs became filled with photos instead of drawings. And these days if your house burns down, it's a TV camera that appears to record your personal tragedy for tomorrow's news.

As that army of illustrators found fewer paying jobs, they began to leave the field, and illustrations in books became more rare. And when cheap paperbacks began to appear in the 1920s and 1930s, publishers began to do away with images altogether. After a while, images were reserved only for the fanciest editions. After all, photographs in a novel would be weird, right?

And yet, when we hand books without pictures to children for the first time, we never tell the story about cameras. We never mention new technologies and market forces. Instead we make up lies. And what's worse, we've begun to believe our own lies. Some people actually think that real adults don't want pictures in their stories, which means that only immature people would want to read graphic novels or manga. They actually think that images in stories rob us of our imagination.

How crazy is that? All readers use their imagination. Yes, when you read a novel with no pictures, you have to imagine what the characters look like. But when you read a comic book, for example, you still have to conjure up how characters speak, how they move, what they're thinking. You infer the passage of time because some panels last a split second, while others represent an entire month passing. You imagine the heat and dampness of a jungle setting, the noise of a freight train, the angry rush of being betrayed.

Pictures don't rob us of any of the emotions and meanings that stories create. How could they?

So the next time someone looks at your comic books, graphic novels, or manga and says, "Those books have pictures. Aren't they for little kids? Don't you like to use your imagination?" now you know how to reply . . .

People didn't get imaginations in 1910. They got cameras. The lack of pictures in contemporary novels does not have to do with reader maturity, but with an economic shift a hundred years ago, the replacement of the hand-drawn world by a new technology. Pictures disappeared from books not to match readers' tastes or abilities, but to save money. Imagination doesn't wither when you read narratives with pictures; it just takes on different forms. And the stories we tell ourselves about what young people and adults want and need and love in their books are based not on reality, but on a lie.

Scott Westerfeld is the author of eighteen novels for young adults, including the Uglies series and *Leviathan*. He splits his time between Sydney and New York City. Scott recently took the essay portion of the SAT test and scored a six.

CHARACTER ANALYSIS / PERSUASIVE ESSAY

Put yourself in the shoes of "the villain" and write an essay from his
or her perspective.

It's On Like Donkey Kong

by **ALAN GRATZ**

Super. That's what they call him now. *Super* Mario. There he is
on magazine covers and cereal boxes and fan sites—red overalls
gleaming, bushy mustache waving in the breeze, white-gloved
fist pumping in victory. The Hero of the Mushroom Kingdom.
How many times is he supposed to have saved the princess
now? Even I've lost count, and a bunch of those times it was me
he beat up to "rescue" her. That's right. I'm Donkey Kong, the
chest-beating, barrel-throwing, red-tie-wearing giant ape who's
been taking it on my protruding chin from Mario since 1981.
I've been around since the beginning, right from the very start,
and I know the story of the real Mario. The not-so-super Mario
that the Mushroom Kingdom muckety-mucks don't want you
to know about. See, the truth is, Mario's the real villain here,
not me.

You don't believe me? I'm not surprised. Who's going to
believe anything a guy named Donkey Kong says, right? But
see, right there, that's defense exhibit A. You know who gave
me that stupid name? Mario did. That's right. People forget,

but once upon a time I was Mario's pet gorilla. Don't ask me what some average Joe carpenter-turned-plumber is doing with a giant Eastern lowland gorilla for a pet, but that's where all this started. And what does this genius name me? "Donkey Kong." Really, Mario? Only a true villain would demean his own pet like that! How is anybody supposed to take me seriously? But, you know, maybe that was the point. If you got to name your own arch-nemesis, you'd give him a silly name too, wouldn't you? You think Darth Vader would be so scary if Luke Skywalker got to name him "Darth Donkey"?

But Mario's history of verbal abuse is nothing compared to his pattern of physical abuse. The guy used to whip me. While I was trapped in a cage with nowhere to go. That's why I escaped in the first place. And, yeah, I snatched up his girlfriend Pauline and carried her to the top of a building. A little cliché, I know. King Kong pulled that stunt back in the thirties, but what can I say? I'm a traditionalist. All I really wanted to do was get her someplace Mario couldn't touch her. I wasn't kidnapping her because I was in love with her. Come on. I'm an eight-hundred-pound gorilla. She's a blond bombshell. I'm not her type and she's not mine. But given Mario's history of getting rough with his pets (i.e., me), I was worried about her. There were days Pauline would come to visit me wearing sunglasses to hide a black eye, or long sleeves to cover her bruises. Her boyfriend Mario had a temper that put Bowser's to shame. You know Bowser, that big spiky turtle guy with the horns who looks like he just swallowed a stinky old sock? He's a brute, all right, but he's got nothing on Mario when it comes to being the king of cruel.

But it wasn't just that Mario was mean. He was thoughtless. The guy jumps over barrels, dodges fireballs, rides conveyor belts, and tears out rivets—making buildings unsafe and not up to code anymore, by the way—and knocks me down on my head to get his girlfriend back. But then what does he do? He dumps her! One minute he's all, "Take your stinking paws off Pauline, you dirty ape!" and the next minute he's jumping down a sewer pipe to rescue another woman, Princess Peach. It's like Theseus braving the labyrinth, slaying the Minotaur, and winning the love of Ariadne, only to dump her on Naxos on the way home. Off Mario goes into the Mushroom Kingdom after Princess Peach like she's Helen of Troy or something, and poor Pauline is all but forgotten. Then later, he forgets all about Princess Peach and hooks up with Princess Daisy before handing *her* off to his brother Luigi when he's done with her. Everybody in the Mushroom Kingdom sees how badly Mario treats his women, but you know how it is: Ladies love the bad boys. Me, Bowser, Wario (Mario's supposedly "evil" cousin)—we've all tried to do the right thing and keep Mario's women from getting hurt, but Mario always comes jumping, squashing, fireballing, and smashing his way back.

And while we're on the subject of the smashing and the squashing, let's have a moment of silence for all the little animals Mario has killed. Turtles? They're practically extinct in the Mushroom Kingdom after Mario ran around jumping on them with both feet and kicking them around like soccer balls. And goombas? Those cute little mushroom guys? This is the Mushroom Kingdom. It's like the goomba promised land down there. And here comes Mario, some *paesano* from the surface world, hopping around flattening them indiscriminately. I mean, these goombas are just on their way to work or to the grocery store or back home to see their little goomba kids, and Mario stomps on them like they're cockroaches. And Yoshi? That cute green dinosaur thing? Mario doesn't kill him. No. He just rides him around like a horse. Yoshi is a sentient creature, people! The other Yoshis live peacefully in villages and have town hall meetings on Yoshi Island, for goomba's sake! It's like if an American ran across a Canadian on the street and just hopped on his back and started riding him around. 'Cause, you know, why not? He's just a Canadian.

Look, the history books are written by the winners. And Mario? He's a winner. Axes, lava, enormous bullets, man-eating plants—no matter what you throw at this guy, he finds a way to beat you and get the girl. Then he looks like a hero, and you look like a big dumb bad guy when it's really the other way around. When are people going to start seeing Mario for what he really is? Take another look beyond the Mario party line, my friends. You might just be surprised at what you find.

But, hey, don't listen to me. I'm just the eight-hundred-pound gorilla in the room.

Alan Gratz has been battling Donkey Kong since he was nine years old. When he's not playing one of his six video game consoles, he writes books for young readers, including *Samurai Shortstop, The Brooklyn Nine,* and *Fantasy Baseball.*

PERSONAL ESSAY

If time travel were possible, what moments from your past would you revisit and change? Where would you go in the future and what would you do?

The World Is Full of Time Machines

by STEVE ALMOND

If you had told me back in high school that scientists would soon invent a tiny portable device that could call any phone on earth or visit any website, I would have said, "You are a very crazy person. Also, what is a website?"

Technology is basically magic, and it continually generates new and far-fetched realities, such as men bouncing on the moon and toothpastes that change color based on the weather. The holy grail, when it comes to technology, is the creation of a time machine. And if you talk to the right folks, they'll tell you time travel is totally possible. All you have to do is build a spaceship that travels close to the speed of light, zoom into space, then zoom back. Because objects age more slowly at high speeds, you would travel thousands of years into the earth's future.

You got that? All you need is a spaceship that travels close to the speed of light.

But the truth is that you don't need a fancy spaceship to time travel. You don't even need technology because human beings are, by our very nature, time travelers. Evolution has endowed us with the two essential tools: imagination and memory.

This is why, when I eat mint chip ice cream, and in particular when I eat mint chip ice cream with hot caramel sauce, I am instantly transported back to the summer of 1981 and I am sitting in Edy's Ice Cream Parlor in the Town & Country Mall with a girl named Sharon who I want desperately to kiss. Sharon is patiently explaining to me why that is not going to happen, not now and not ever, and I am responding not with words—there's nothing to say, really—but by shoveling mint chip ice cream and caramel sauce into my mouth. It's all there: the caramel sticking to my teeth, my wretched black angora sweater, the sunlight lancing through the storefront window, even the sickly scent of the cologne, Jacomo, in which I have doused myself.

Do I want to be back there? The answer should be no. But human beings are complicated creatures. We have a tendency to return to the scene of our humiliations, in much the same way a dog returns to a cruel master.

Then again, we also spend a lot of time trolling the past for moments of glory. I will admit, though not happily, that I listen to the song "Don't Stop Believin'" by the band Journey for the simple reason that doing so reminds me of slow-dancing with Juliet, the first girl who not only allowed me to kiss her, but seemed eager to reciprocate. I am inordinately fond of cherry lip gloss for the same reason.

As for time travel into the future, I do that every single day.

If my favorite football team, the Oakland Raiders, is playing on Sunday, I devote hours to envisioning how the game will play out, often before I actually get out of bed. And though I know the Raiders are almost guaranteed to lose the game in a heartbreaking fashion, in my version they always manage to pull it out.

The same pattern prevails whenever I have to deliver a speech. I see myself in front of the audience and my hair looks fantastic and my shirt hangs just right and I look genuinely humble during the standing ovation.

You can certainly argue at this point that what I'm describing isn't genuine time travel. But let's consider for a moment what would happen if you were able to travel through time. Say you wound up five hundred years into the future. The whole thing would be pretty freaky for a while, what with all the robots around to floss your teeth and the Internet chip implanted in your brain.

At a certain point, though, what had been the future would just become your present. It would just be life. You would get up in the morning and think about what happened yesterday, or last week, or when you were fifteen years old, before you became a time traveler. Or you'd think about what was going to happen later in the day, or maybe next week. And the truth is, in those moments, you wouldn't be living in the present. You'd be time traveling.

This is just what human beings do. It's how we've learned to cope with our giant brains, with the burden of consciousness.

We don't live in our circumstances so much as we live in our dreams and our memories and our regrets.

The various captains of the self-help movement—from yoga gurus to celebrity psychologists—consider these forms of time travel just terrible. They feel we should all live "in the moment." But our present moments are often painful or confusing or tedious. It strikes me as perfectly natural, and perhaps even heroic in some cases, to look ahead or back, to anticipate or savor.

Upstairs, in my office, is a photo of Rich Gannon, my favorite Raiders player, dancing past a defender and into the end zone. Whenever I look at that picture I think about Gannon and his astonishing grace and how the Raiders used to be great. And I think about how they might be great again, and what next year will bring. And downstairs, in my basement, I have three thousand compact discs, which my wife would very much like me to throw away.

But every time I head down, intending to do so, I wind up putting one on the stereo and dancing through all the memories it unleashes.

The world is full of time machines.

You can fight that truth. Or you can ride.

Steve Almond is the author of ten books of fiction and nonfiction, most recently the story collection *God Bless America*. He lives outside Boston with his wife and two kids, and his hobbies include writing, reading, and dreaming up new candy bars.

PERSONAL ESSAY / GRAPHIC ESSAY

If you could pick any name for yourself, what would it be and why?

Hello. My Name Is

by JENNIFER LOU

BabyNameWizard.com charts Jennifer as *the* most popular girl's name in the 1970s, the decade I was born.

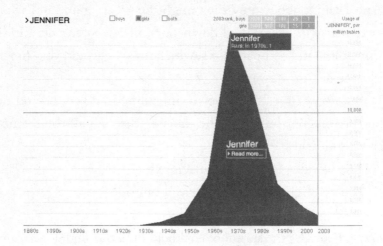

There were so many people in my high school named Jen that I learned to not respond to it unless my last name followed.

To understand how I got my name, you'll need to know the

name of everyone else in my family. When my father came to the United States from China, he chose the name Nelson for reasons he can no longer remember. I like to think it's after Nelson Mandela or even Willie Nelson, but it's more likely that it's because his Chinese name, Neng-Yin, also begins and ends with an N. When my parents had their first child, they wanted his name to start with that same letter. They also wanted something unique. My brother's English name is Norbert. BabyNameWizard.com shows that Norbert topped the charts at number 222 in 1920. It wasn't even in the top one thousand in the 1970s, the decade he was born.

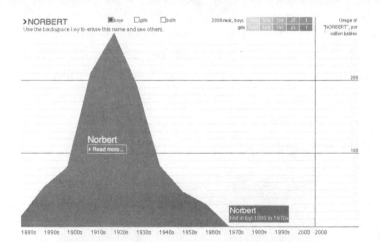

My parents also chose Norbert because of its meaning: northern brightness. It's Germanic in origin. Two years and ten months after my brother's arrival, I was born. By then, my mother had learned that you could never buy souvenirs with the name Norbert on them.

My mom's chosen English name is Julie. So when I was born a girl, they scoured the baby name book for popular "J" names. And they fell in love with the name Jennifer for both its popularity and meaning: the fair one. What my mom hadn't anticipated was that because the name was so popular, souvenirs with my name were often sold out.

So my full name is Jennifer Lou. No middle name. Nothing. Everyone else in my family has their Chinese name as their English middle name. It's on official documents, passports, licenses, and in my brother's case, his birth certificate. The middle name field on my birth certificate? Blank. A parental oversight because they hadn't made the time to select a Chinese name.

CERTIFICATE OF LIVE BI H
VS-2 Rev. 10 73

CONNECTICUT STATE DEPARTMENT OF HEALTH
79 ELM ST., HARTFORD, CONN. 06115

(State File No.)

1. Child's name (First) Jennifer	(Middle)	(Last) Lou
2. Weight	3. Sex	4. Place of Birth	5. Date of Birth

Having no middle name is even more significant when you grow up in white, middle-class Connecticut where everyone has one. It was a rough childhood. Not only did I have to learn how to ski, how to play tennis, and how to tie sweaters around my neck, I also had to navigate Puritan New England middle name–less. "You're incomplete!" friends would say.

I took matters into my own hands. When I started seventh grade at Sage Park Middle School, I enrolled as Jennifer Elizabeth Lou. I picked Elizabeth because it was the whitest name I could think of. And, my God, I wanted to be white because in Windsor, Connecticut, where less than one percent of the population was Chinese, white, to me, meant belonging. It meant being pretty and popular, and that boys would like me. I had it in my head that they didn't like me because I was Chinese. Different. But really, they didn't like me because I was ugly.

This is my seventh grade yearbook photo. The antithesis of delicate and fair. Notice the layered, 'fro-like perm, the buck teeth, and fangs. Thankfully, the black-and-white photo softens some of my brilliant fashion choices: a cantaloupe-colored T-shirt with concrete gray collars and a smoking hot, pink pair of glasses, thicker than a Coke bottle.

By ninth grade, I was ready to shed my inner white Elizabeth, mainly because I thought the initials JEL looked stupid. I returned to plain Jennifer Lou, and I started to like that I didn't have a middle name. I liked that I was the only one in the family whose Chinese name wasn't their English middle name. I was two separate entities.

My Chinese name is 陸琬玗 (Lù Wǎn Yú). One May I asked, "Mom, what does my Chinese name mean?"

"What?" she said, annoyed. "It doesn't mean anything."

"Well, what's Norb's Chinese name mean then? Also nothing?"

"Oh, no, his name means 'joy to the world.'"

Of course it does.

I later pressed for more clarification. I discovered why my Chinese name never became my English middle name. When I was born, my mom didn't have a Chinese name picked out for me. Instead, my mom sent all my birth information back to Taiwan to a Chinese astrologer. She needed to know what elements to include in my name based on my birth details. If you know nothing else about Taiwanese culture, know that they are crazy superstitious. You can't leave rice uneaten on your plate, put your chopsticks standing up in a bowl, give an umbrella or knives as gifts—and your daughter can't be named without an astrologer.

The astrologer said that my name needed jade. This is the character for jade:

玉

This is a common variation of the character for jade:

王

In Chinese culture, jade is said to possess the five essential virtues of Chinese philosophy: compassion, modesty, courage, justice, and wisdom. Virtues she thought I might need when trying to be "the fair one." So, as she created my name, my mom weaved as much jade as possible.

Lù, my last name, means land:

陸

Wǎn means gentle, gracious. Wǎn is traditionally written with the female root:

婉

But Mom took it out and swapped in the jade root:

琬

Yú is an antiquated version of the character for jade:

玗

I guess that makes my Chinese name mean "the land of gentle jade." Pretty lame compared to "joy to the world," if you ask me.

So that is how I ended up with two names: a simple English name, and a customized Chinese one. Actually, if you count my nicknames, I have at least fifteen names. They range from obvious abbreviations like J-Lou to more story-oriented ones like Gimpy, Potty Lou, and Evil.

Then there are the nicknames that reflect my stage in life. Five years ago, in the midst of a post-breakup, mid-career crisis, I came to a realization. There was no point in trying to be something I wasn't (white) or something others wanted me to be (the fair one). I started making mass changes in my life— challenging old, traditional beliefs from my past, particularly the negative, self-destructive ones, and exploring new and healthier trains of thought. When you clean house and tear down that Great Wall, it's easy to second-guess what you're doing. But I persevered, and through it, I gained a greater sense of confidence. I started feeling free to be myself, enough so that the spunk and spark returned to my life, enough so that a good friend started calling me "Jen 2.0." I would spit out a sassy, witty comment and he would hiss, "Watch out! It's Jen 2.0!"

I had become a newer, speedier, more enhanced version of

the old me. And I began to love my names for what they are, for what they aren't, and for the betweenness that they capture. Because I finally learned to love the uniqueness that is me.

So if you're ever in the market for a name, drop me a line; my family knows a good astrologer.

Jennifer Lou is a writer in San Francisco who chronicles life as an ABC (American born Chinese). She founded LitUp Writers, a local humor storytelling series, and works at Coliloquy, a digital publisher. When she's not serving on the board of Youth Speaks, Jen plays with sea otters at the Monterey Bay Aquarium under the ruse of being a volunteer.

PERSUASIVE ESSAY

Make an argument in favor of something you care about. Then make a convincing
counterargument addressing that same topic.

Breakfast on Mars: Why We Should Colonize the Red Planet (Part 1. Argument)

by **CHRIS HIGGINS**

Imagine waking up on Mars. You'd look up at a yellowish-brown sky and see the sun rise much as it does on Earth. As you roll out of bed, there'd be a spring in your step, because gravity on Mars is only one-third as strong as it is on Earth. You might check to see what had happened on Earth while you slept—but more likely, you'd sit down for breakfast with your fellow colonists (Martians, all of you) and plan for another day building your civilization on Mars.

Humans have always ventured into new lands, exploring every inch of our first globe, Earth, and sometimes settling in dangerous and bizarre places. We even have a research base with over a thousand people in Antarctica! Yet, Earth now has seven billion people, and we're quickly running out of room. When we do, the next logical place to go is Mars. While it is far away and the journey is dangerous, the expedition to Mars is no riskier than what our ancestors faced when making their own migrations across land and sea.

When we look back at the twentieth century, there's one obvious milestone that stands out for our species as a whole: We left Earth for the first time and even sent people to the moon. (Though only a dozen walked on the surface, and they were all men.) In the twenty-first century, Mars can and should be our next milestone. And when we go, it will likely be a one-way trip, like the Pilgrims of Plymouth Rock took to "the New World"—space travel is too expensive, time-consuming, and hazardous to expect that a person might go to Mars and come back to Earth. Just making a one-way trip takes between six months and a year. The journey could become less grueling, however, as we learn more about space travel and spaceship construction (just as international travel is commonplace today but was incredibly difficult for the Pilgrims). In any case, once you have reached a new world, why would you want to go back?

In 1962, President John F. Kennedy, Jr., gave a speech at Rice University that kicked off the race to put men on the moon. JFK told the American people we should go to the moon, "not because [it is] easy, but because [it is] hard." As a society, we need to challenge ourselves to do what is hard in order to make progress. If we simply choose the easy stuff, we'll never achieve anything great. Getting to the moon was arduous—eight American astronauts died in training accidents. But what we gained from the mission to the moon was immense: safety gear for firefighters and race car drivers, freeze-dried food used for soldiers' rations, and even technology that powers credit card transactions. We had no idea all those inventions would spring from the lunar missions, but now they're part of daily life. What's more, Americans were inspired by the challenge of putting men on the moon, and that inspiration drove a generation of innovators to try what was previously thought impossible. It is no coincidence that about a decade after the moon landing, personal computers appeared in living rooms; the technology we needed for small computers was another direct result of our trip to the moon. Achieving JFK's vision of landing men on the moon was valuable because it was hard. The challenge today is to put men and women on Mars.

Yes, there are easier things we could do in space. We could put a base on the moon or continue to build the International Space Station. But the biggest problem with those goals is that there's nothing inspirational about them—we have already launched satellites and visited the moon, over and over, and there isn't much more to learn. What's worse, the moon has very little water, it doesn't have an atmosphere (so it's unbelievably cold), the soil is basically dust (Don't try to grow anything on the lunar surface.), and the moon's days and nights last about a month (Would you like to be in sunlight or darkness for a month at a time?). It's just not a suitable place for people to live. By comparison, Mars has some water (frozen in the ground, like permafrost on Earth), a thin atmosphere and soil (so crops could grow), and it has days and nights much like Earth. In other words, although Mars is far away, very cold, and devoid of life, it is actually *possible* to live there. Because we can sustain a settlement in Antarctica here on Earth, it stands to reason that we could do the same on Mars.

As we look to the future, we need to plan for our children, and their children, and there simply isn't enough room on Earth to keep growing as we have. By establishing a colony on Mars, we open up an entire planet's worth of room for people to live. This is the single best land investment we can make, especially since there is hardly any unclaimed land left on Earth, no stretch of new frontier into which we can explore. Mars is there for the taking. And what's most enticing is that we could actually put humans on Mars within a few decades. Elon Musk (creator of PayPal and founder of the space exploration company SpaceX) says he plans to retire on Mars. His retirement is only about twenty years away. It's easy to imagine what this means—people will be on Mars, and soon. Wouldn't you like to be one of them?

When you get ready for bed in your Martian bedroom, you might look to the stars and search for what the astronomer Carl Sagan called "the pale blue dot" known as Earth. And as you do, it's likely that your cousins back on Earth will do the same, looking up at the same night sky for a twinkling red dot and wondering when the next spaceship will blast off, bound for Mars.

PERSUASIVE ESSAY

Make an argument in favor of something you care about. Then make a convincing
counterargument addressing that same topic.

Robots Only: Why We Shouldn't Colonize Mars[9] (Part 2. Counterargument)

by CHRIS HIGGINS

Everyone is curious about Mars, our red neighbor in the solar system. We want to know how much water is there, and we want to dig into Martian rocks, looking for fossils of life that may have existed in the distant past. It is true that to get this information, we need to have some presence on the ground there. But just because we're curious about a place certainly does not mean we should try to colonize it. Humans have a tendency to want to take over. But we need to resist this urge. We already have a planet that's perfectly suited to our needs; we should leave Mars as the domain of creatures that can exist happily upon its freezing, barren landscape. We should get out of the way and leave Mars to the robots.

The main reason to visit Mars is to learn more about its past. We want to uncover information about its climate and

---

9 This essay is inspired by the scholarly paper "Fast, Cheap and Out of Control: A Robot Invasion of the Solar System" by MIT scientists Rodney A. Brooks and Anita M. Flynn, published in the *Journal of the British Interplanetary Society*, vol. 42, pp. 478–485, 1989. Please read the paper for more specifics on building robots for space exploration.

history (Was it once like Earth but then dried up?), we want to map its surface, and we yearn to know whether there is, or ever was, life on Mars. Given what researchers have learned so far, the best we can hope for is small life, maybe no bigger than bacteria—which is not nearly as exciting as the dinosaurs and other fossils we find on Earth—but it would still change our outlook on the universe to know that Mars had played host to living organisms. If Mars had life, we could assume that life is everywhere, and we are not alone. Yet, when we think about our desire to further understand Mars, we must accept that robots have taught us everything we have learned thus far about this planet, and it should remain that way moving forward.

As I write this essay (in early 2012), two robotic rovers are already sitting on Mars, hibernating during the Martian winter. The twin rovers are called Spirit and Opportunity, and they arrived on Mars way back in January 2004. They were designed for a mission lasting only 90 sols (Days are called "sols" on Mars.), but the rovers lasted far longer than expected—Spirit finally failed in 2010 (six years after its initial mission ended), and Opportunity is still running. These two rovers, along with satellites armed with cameras and other gear, have given us an up-close view of Mars—something we can't do well using telescopes on Earth. And what's remarkable is that they've done the job cheaply, by space exploration standards. Spirit and Opportunity have so far cost about $900 million, which is the cost of two shuttle launches.

NASA has proven that robots work well on the red planet.

In addition to the two rovers, a larger rover called Curiosity is currently en route to Mars, and will be there by the time you read this. Because we're so good at building and launching robots, it makes sense to stick with the program. What's more, if we did build a permanent human settlement on Mars, we might be tempted to ignore our own environmental problems on Earth. It might not seem as bad to ruin Earth's forests or to use up our drinking water if we had a new planet available to colonize. The reality is, even if we did send some people to Mars, we couldn't send everybody.

The most costly parts of space missions are building things to send into space, and then launching them. Humans are very heavy—we're basically big, weighty bags of water—and the life-support systems needed to keep us alive are heavy too. We need food, we need liquid, and we need air to breathe. But robots don't have lives that need support, and they can be built at any imaginable size or weight. Furthermore, designing life-support systems for long-term human colonies requires lots of unbelievably expensive experiments. The enormous Biosphere 2 experiment in Arizona (3.14 acres in size—the same number as pi) was partly envisioned as one such test for a human settlement on Mars. Yet, after twenty years in operation, it is now considered a massive failure. (Today, it has been converted into a research center and tourist destination focused on a better understanding of Earth, not life outside our planet.) Robots don't have any of these requirements or need for biospheres; our rovers already wander the surface of Mars just fine.

What's more, when a robot breaks, it doesn't die. Robots can be fixed or replaced. But with humans, any major problem with a spacecraft or life-support equipment means almost certain death for astronauts, which would demoralize a nation. If we sent humans to Mars and they died due to some glitch, we would be devastated, and might never send humans to Mars again, out of fear of a repeat failure. But no one is *that* sad when we watch our current Martian rovers slowly fall apart (as wheels and batteries fail over time). The rovers have done their jobs well, and eventually all machines wear out. When the rovers finally break down for good, they'll sit right where they stopped—and someday other rovers might visit them. Losing a robot isn't the same thing as losing an astronaut. Robots don't have families.

Also, robots, as opposed to humans, are not emotionally needy. Humans like to drive; we like the feeling of control even when it's unwarranted. But does our overbearing nature always lead to progress? Not necessarily. Not only should we send robots to Mars instead of humans, but we also need to remember that, once there, it is better to let them do their work without interfering. Right now, we try to control our robots by having human operators on Earth send careful instructions to our robot explorers. This gives us a pleasant feeling of control, but it is a waste of the robots' time. Mars is really far away, and even at the speed of light, there will always be a delay. In fact, it takes radio waves (our remote control signals) anywhere from three to twenty-one minutes to reach Mars, depending on where the planets are in their orbits. There is no way to change this. So if you send a signal that says "turn left," it takes at least three minutes to get there and another three minutes for the "okay" signal to come back. This makes "driving" the rovers painfully slow, and it reduces the amount of work rovers can do as they wait around for instructions. Robots are now smart enough to figure things out without so much help. Thus, we need to let go of this control-freak mind-set and let the rovers do their own work, on their own schedule, only checking in when there's something to tell us (like sending back pictures or other information). We need to stop pretending that the robots are stand-ins for humans. No need to get emotional. They are there to serve a singular purpose: so we can learn.

Sending humans to Mars and building a settlement for them would be a colossal waste of money and would entail terrible danger for our astronauts, our space program, and our own planet. Earth is our home, and here we should stay. But we can—and should—send our robot emissaries to Mars and beyond, to learn and to send back pictures, sounds, and data of places where human feet may never tread.

Chris Higgins is a writer living in Portland, Oregon. His work has appeared in *This American Life*, *Mental Floss* magazine, and the *Portland Mercury*. In his spare time, he enjoys photography and documentary films.

Recall and Defend

by RITA WILLIAMS-GARCIA

If you've experienced a brush with history, wouldn't your account of that event be accurate above all others? Memory itself
can be a tricky, fleeting, subjective ghost, hard to pin down
with absolute certainty, especially if there is no hard evidence
of the event. But a person's own account of their footnote in
history is more than mere memory; it is their truer-than-not
story to tell.

Of course, certain factors would come into play about the
"recaller" and the event. For example, the recaller's age and
relative state of mind at the time of the event should be considered. A very young child might have to defer to an older sibling
or parent's recollection since the recaller's ability to access, associate, and express details go a long way in re-creating the event
and convincing listeners that she or he was actually there. It
also helps if the recaller saw her encounter as a significant one
at the time of the event. How else would she consciously or
subconsciously store the event into memory, say, longer than

she'd store a textbook chapter's worth of material needed to pass Friday's exam?

Put my father, my sister, and me together at a family gathering and sooner or later the argument would follow about my first and only encounter with a Kennedy.

In early spring of 1968, I took a picture with Senator Robert F. Kennedy at Monterey Airport. In my father and sister's version, the senator picked me up and held me as we posed for the picture, while I maintain that we just stood side by side. We are fine with all the details of that day except for the actual contact between the senator and me. No matter how much doubt I express that the senator picked me up, this is the highlight of my father and sister's recollection.

On their side, they outnumber me, two to one. (My mother and brother never took sides. They left the debating to us.) They are older than I am, and in my family, age equals reliability. "What do you know? You weren't but a sprout," my father, twenty-four years my senior, would say. My sister, Rosalind, who outranks me by two years, would agree. They were there. They knew what they saw, because, according to them, they were older and therefore clearer than I was at the time.

Also on their side, both dad and Rosalind are, in the Williams tradition, natural-born storytellers, able to keep a listener hooked with detail, story rhythm, and humor—the humor at my expense. They've told the RFK story every year, hitting the familiar high points while maintaining their version. I too am a Williams, but by my family's standards, I'm no storyteller.

So, if my father and sister corroborate each other, were present at the event, remain firm on what they saw, and they can repeat their account in detail and rhythm, why then can't I just go along with their version?

That day, I wrote in my diary, "3/23/68—I saw Robert Kennedy in person at the airport." Three months later I wrote, "6/5/68—Kennedy won the Calif. victory but Serhan Seran (sic) shot him in the head" followed by "6/6/68—Kennedy died." Our famous meeting happened three weeks before my eleventh birthday. I was younger than my sister and father, but I knew who Robert F. Kennedy was. Although my diary entries were without particular flourish, I knew at the time our meeting was significant. I made a conscious effort to retain my interest in the senator, having written three entries of him in my diary, when I could have easily used those lines to write about episodes of my favorite TV shows, *That Girl* and *Garrison's Gorillas*.

This is what I recall from that day: It was a blustery kite-flying day in March. Instead of pulling weeds in the front yard, as we did every Saturday, my sister, brother, and I dressed in our school clothes and drove to Monterey Airport with our parents to hear Senator Robert F. Kennedy deliver a presidential campaign speech. His bangs flapped as he spoke to the crowd. From his speech, I can only recall the senator saying how young men were old enough to die for their country while fighting in Vietnam, but they weren't old enough to vote in their own country's elections. The senator might have spoken about poverty and racial inequality. I don't remember. But what he said about young men dying in Vietnam struck a chord with me because I was standing next to my father who had just come home from Vietnam and was very much alive. This is the only part of Kennedy's speech I can attest to with certainty. My father and sister do not include any of Kennedy's speech in their account.

When he finished, he exited to his left with a small group of men surrounding him. My father grabbed my hand, and we went running to our right toward the senator. I remember he wore a tan-colored raincoat. My father said something to one of the men in the senator's entourage and within seconds I had taken a picture with Robert Kennedy. If he spoke two words to me I couldn't tell you what they were.

It is a plain account, but it is what I remember. Forty years later, I maintain doubt that the senator picked me up. At nearly eleven, I was four foot eight and weighed between seventy-five and ninety pounds. I was simply too old and too big to be lifted in someone's arms as if I were five. I was also an avowed tomboy who flexed her muscles at every opportunity. The humiliation of being picked up like a baby in a public place, with a photograph to document the act, would have haunted me like a bad prom night.

Unlike my sister and father, I can't say he didn't pick me up, yet I feel strongly that it was unlikely. While they might have seen the event, I both saw and experienced my brush with fame. My recall isn't rhythmic, captivating storytelling in the

Williams tradition, but it is an earnest, unvarnished account with both minor and pointed details. Furthermore, I'm not afraid to admit which details I have no recollection of. It is the comingling of the concrete with the fleeting that compels me to believe my version is nearer to the truth than a more climactic story version of it. It is my version that allows me to remember my personal history and who I was at age eleven.

To date, there is no indisputable evidence to support either version. Specifically, there is no photograph of the senator and me. My father has since passed, but his version lives on through my sister. At every other family gathering.

I am resigned. I must outlive my sister so that my recollection is the only surviving family account of my brush with fame. After all, it is my memory. All mine. I'll tell it how I remember it.

Rita Williams-Garcia is the *New York Times* bestselling author of eight novels for young adults and middle grade readers. Her recent novels, *Jumped* and *One Crazy Summer*, were named National Book Award finalists. *One Crazy Summer* was also named a Coretta Scott King Award winner, a Newbery Honor Book, and a Scott O'Dell Award winner. Rita lives in Jamaica, New York, has two adult daughters, and is on the faculty at the Vermont College of Fine Arts Writing for Children & Young Adults MFA Program.

PERSONAL ESSAY

Write about a before and after. What was life like before? What was life like after?

My Life Before Television

by ELIZABETH WINTHROP

I grew up so long ago that we didn't have a television in our house until I was thirteen years old. What I did have were three brothers. I was squashed in the middle of them: first came Joe, then Ian, then me, and last Stewart. I ended up with five brothers, but the younger two were born so much later that they not only had a television, they had a color one.

It wasn't until much later that I learned the more television we watched, the fewer adventures we seemed to have.

We lived in Washington, D.C. My father was a reporter who worked from home. Every week he had to write articles about the famous people in town. Senators and spies and ambassadors were always coming to our house so my father could interview them. Sometimes they came for dinner, and sometimes they just sat in the living room while my father asked them questions and took notes and glared at us if we got anywhere near or made any noise.

This was the time when everybody was worried that the

Soviet Union (which is what Russia was called back then) might drop a bomb on the White House. We lived only ten miles from the White House, so my father was always asking questions about what plans our government was making to defend us, and people all over the country talked about building bomb shelters in case the government wasn't making any plans.

My oldest brother, Joe, was our boss, the leader, the one who told us what to do and when to do it. The rest of us went along with him mainly because the projects he came up with were usually pretty interesting. He was a kind of genius who seemed to know everything about everything. He was a math genius, a chemist, and an electrical engineer. Down in the basement of our house, he'd taken over three rooms and filled them with his chemistry set, a Bunsen burner, electrical equipment that dangled from the ceiling, and an oscilloscope that measured the exact wave shape of an electrical signal. I had no idea why we had to measure wave shapes, but I was perfectly happy to turn the dials and watch the green dot grow into a line and bounce up and down across the screen. That's because it was the closest thing we had to a television.

We begged and begged our parents to buy us a TV, but they kept saying no. When we got really desperate, we went down the street and watched our friend Jack's TV even though the picture was brown and had a weird spot like a bubble that wandered around in the middle. But never mind. We were watching TV. We were like the other kids at school. We were up on the latest.

Then suddenly, my father began to get requests to speak on television news programs about all those politicians and presidents and congressmen he was always interviewing and bingo, one day, we came home and we had a TV right there in our very own house.

We were hooked. Our TV was the latest model and had good reception and no weird brown spot in the middle of the screen. Once we turned it on, we pretty much never turned it off. When we got home from school and on the weekends, we sat there watching shows like *Leave It to Beaver* and *Gunsmoke*. After we got that TV, my parents didn't seem to care how much we watched it.

Now I know why.

Here's what we weren't doing because we got a television.

We were no longer down in our secret office in the basement mixing strange chemicals together from my brother's chemistry set and producing satisfying explosions and sometimes small bombs that rerouted the stream at the bottom of our hill. We were no longer catching the crayfish and salamanders that popped up to the surface of the stream after we'd set off the bomb, and carrying them up to our room in glass bowls and leaving them there for days so that their water turned all murky and began to smell.

We were no longer running across the roof between our bedrooms so we could sneak into each other's rooms through the windows. We were no longer trying to squeeze into the very small but enticing space under the first floor bathroom, and my brother Joe was no longer stuck in there between the pipes, which meant my parents no longer had to call the plumber in to turn off the water and saw through one of the copper pipes to get him out.

We were no longer digging enormous holes in the front yard such as the fourteen-foot bomb shelter. We had television now, so we didn't need to be outside instructing all the neighborhood kids on how to use the very special bucket system Joe had designed so that a full bucket of dirt careening down the hill on a wire track pulled up an empty bucket, which also meant we didn't have to haul the heavy red clay around on swampy summer days. This is the same hole my parents completely ignored until we showed them the big room we'd dug out at the bottom so that the family could spend the night down there if a bomb did hit the White House. This is the same hole my father then had covered over with a very heavy wooden lid built by a carpenter who charged him a lot of money, just to be sure that no neighborhood kid ever fell down our hole. This is the same hole that meant my parents had to pay higher insurance premiums in case some neighborhood kid managed to move aside this incredibly heavy wooden lid and fall down our very special, now entirely off-limits hole, and crack his or her head and never get out and die down there in the middle of our old comic books and used-up soda cans.

But who cared? We had television now. Instead of listening to the Lone Ranger calling "Hi-ho Silver" on the radio, we could actually see the masked man and his faithful sidekick,

Tonto, right there on our television screen. This meant we no longer went down into the storm sewers to run a private telephone line from our house to Al's house to Jack's house to Rich's house, so that we could have conversations that grownups knew nothing about. After all, if you have parents who insist on closing down a perfectly good bomb shelter you've spent all summer digging, then you can't trust them not to listen in on your other plans.

But soon, our friends were all over at our house watching our television because it wasn't brown and it didn't have that strange bubble in the middle of the screen, so I guess we didn't need to call them on our private phone line anyway.

And because of television, we were no longer taping our parents' dinner conversations with very important people from the government just because my father had bet my brother fifty dollars that he couldn't actually wiretap our dining room. This also meant my brother wasn't as rich, because he was no longer able to make that easy fifty dollars by playing an entire dinner conversation back to my father on his Wollensak reel-to-reel tape recorder. My father was happy because he no longer worried about us running wiretaps into his home office or the living room where he interviewed presidents and senators and even John Glenn the astronaut, because we were too busy watching another season of *I Love Lucy* or *Have Gun—Will Travel*.

The sad thing was that years later, when I decided to write a particular essay about my childhood and I needed to recall interesting, unique adventures from my own life, I had to write about all the things we did BEFORE we got a television. I wonder now how many other escapades my brothers and I might have pulled off had my father never brought that TV home.

Elizabeth Winthrop is the author of more than sixty books for children and adults. These include the award-winning novels *The Castle in the Attic* and *Counting on Grace*, and picture books *Dumpy La Rue, Shoes*, and *Maia and the Monster Baby*.

PERSONAL ESSAY / GRAPHIC ESSAY

Write about a time when you had to experience pain in order to get a huge reward.

A Rite of Passage
(and the Importance of Penguin Etiquette)

by CHRIS EPTING

There's a common expression, "No pain, no gain," which means that achievement requires some sort of sacrifice—mental sacrifice, physical sacrifice—something. Little did I know how important that phrase would soon become in my life, all because of an invitation to witness, up close and personal, some of the most fascinating (and loveable) animals on this planet.

When my fourteen-year-old daughter, Claire, and I found out that we were going to Antarctica to visit with and study the emperor penguins, we were thrilled. We had entered and won an essay contest that involved writing about how we, in our own lives, help the natural environment. The grand prize promised an almost unfathomable adventure: three weeks living aboard a Russian icebreaker ship near an icy, remote outpost called Snow Hill Island. Recently, the world's largest colony of emperors, tens of thousands of them, had been discovered there, and we were about to have the privilege of their company.

However, getting to Antarctica is no small feat. It is extremely difficult to fly there, as the official population is zero. But for a few small scientific compounds and bases scattered around the massive continent, there is no human life, and so finding a landing strip to accommodate you is a huge challenge. The few who are lucky enough to visit this most mysterious continent (in our case, approximately seventy passengers I'd describe as seasoned world travelers and perhaps thirty or so staff members, including many scientists) do so by ships like ours, which leave from the bottom tip of South America, from a seaport village called Ushuaia—the southernmost city on Earth.

This is where the "pain" comes in. You see, to reach Antarctica, ships must pass through a notoriously violent area of ocean called the Drake Passage, considered to be the roughest stretch of sea on the planet.

Walls of water thirty, sometimes forty feet high—tremendous towers of dark green, icy waves—continually crashed about our ship for two solid days. We would hold on to a railing inside the ship while being violently tilted to one extreme side, then to the other, and then back again. Over and over and over, nonstop. If not for the belt straps on our cabin bed, we would have flown up in the air as we tried to sleep. Anything (and everything!) in our cabin that was not secured was tossed across the room or straight up into the ceiling.

My daughter and I knew about the Drake Passage and were as mentally prepared as we could be. We knew what waited at the end of the journey—the penguins—and so together we convinced ourselves it was all worth the pain. But as mentally prepared as we were, we also had to be physically aware, as well. One false step might result in a broken leg, arm, or worse. It was important to always watch our footing as we crept to the dining room each day to carefully grab a quick meal before returning to our cabin to ride out the sickening, never-ending storm.

I recall one night when I watched my jacket, which was hanging on a hook from the wall, tilt almost perpendicular to the floor. Though we couldn't always feel the full sensation of what was happening, the jacket did not lie—we were almost completely sideways.

We'd venture out for a quick snack when we got hungry, even though walking down the four flights of narrow stairs was treacherous. I fell down once, a lesson to always use two hands on the railing. Something else we discovered is that by lying down, we were better able to control the effects of the movement. Suffice to say, we spent a good part of crossing the Drake on our stomachs.

It was a wild roller coaster and a severe earthquake all at once. Thankfully, we did not get seasick, though many of our fellow adventurers did. But we certainly felt the pain of fear and the unknown. I started to wonder, "Is this worth it? Will the gain be worth all of this struggle?"

Then in an instant, about two and a half days after entering the Drake Passage, the waters calmed. We had entered the Weddell Sea. For the first time on our journey, we walked out on deck and felt the sweet bite of the cold, clean air on our faces. Nearby we saw towering blue and white icebergs, so many that it looked like a virtual city of ice.

Soon, we noticed small black specks on nearby pieces of floating ice. Emperor penguins! The closer our ship got, the more it seemed as if the animals were welcoming us—some of them actually beating their wings together, as if they were applauding our arrival.

Our ship began to cut through the ice as we got closer to Snow Hill Island. An icebreaker is a powerful craft and the only kind of ship that can reach a destination encased in ice. The front of the vessel rises slightly, then crushes down on the ice, pushes ahead a bit, then repeats the process over and over. The path created by the ship doesn't harm the environment; in fact, moments after the ship eases through, the ice reclaims the path and soon seals over once more.

Before long, we reached our final destination. The ladders were lowered and we were allowed to take our first ice walk. Across the crunchy surface, we could see hundreds of penguins in the distance, watching us as we watched them. Even though the colony was about twenty miles away, our arrival had clearly created some curiosity.

As we learned on board, their interest was to be expected. Penguins are extremely curious and not fearful of humans. After all, they don't really know what we are, and we have done nothing to harm them in this environment, so they really have nothing to be scared of.

The next day, two helicopters that would take us from our ship to the base camp were assembled on the deck of the ship. Because of the Drake Passage, the choppers had to be brought over in pieces or risk being destroyed during the journey.

And then we were off, flying low and fast across the ice until we reached base camp, located about twenty miles from the ship. The base camp was a place to rest and replenish, but not where we spent our nights (our ship served as our sleeping quarters). Interestingly, it was never that cold—just below freezing on most days (colder at night), but a couple of layers and our parkas provided more than enough warmth and protection.

After landing, we were given instructions on "penguin eti-quette" (meaning, how to behave properly among these rare and beautiful creatures). These were the basic rules: You can't touch a penguin, but they can touch you if they'd like. You can't crowd them, but they can crowd you if they so desire. And you always give them the right of way. Beyond those rules, we were free to explore, photograph, and observe to our heart's content.

After we began the two-mile hike over the ice to the penguin colony, the group of passengers (some of whom we became good friends with) split up so that they could enjoy the hike peacefully and privately. My daughter and I felt completely alone in this surreal new world. "Like a *Star Wars* planet," Claire said to me.

And she was right.

Within several hundred yards, little clusters of emperors, perhaps ten or so at a time, greeted us, sliding on their bellies and making their wonderful noises, sort of a nasally squeal.

But the real treat still awaited. Within an hour, we came around the base of a large glacier and heard a distant hum. The sound grew louder, and then what was creating the noise came into view: the colony.

As far as we could see, there were emperor penguins—tens of thousands of them, stretched out to the horizon line. It was breathtaking. Thousands of newly hatched chicks waddled among the adults, vying for attention. The adults gathered together, as if reviewing the troops, and an entire social order began to emerge. They had a system. They were a society.

We found a quiet piece of ice, sat down, and within minutes were surrounded by dozens of curious emperors. They stared at us as intently as we stared at them. In some cases, their beaks were just inches from our noses.

For days, we took the helicopters back and forth to the penguin colony from the ship.

We experienced moments that were indescribably unique and even magical. One day, two adult emperors with their three chicks in tow approached Claire, who was resting on the ice. They left the chicks with her, as if she were the babysitter.

Twenty minutes later they returned to collect the chicks. And I will never forget the penguin that, when I jokingly asked which way back to the helicopters, pointed a wing in the correct direction.

It was as if we had been welcomed into another world by some of the smartest, most curious, and toughest creatures on the planet. Every night aboard our safe and warm ship, we thought about what it takes to survive in Antarctica, an incredibly harsh place, which is actually considered a desert given the lack of precipitation there.

But each day on the ice, we also thought about the Drake Passage, that monstrous body of water we had to endure to get where we were. Over the course of our visit, we came to respect and even revere the power of that sea, and even though we knew we'd be in for a rough ride home, we knew we'd be okay.

We still talk about the penguins, as I'm sure we always will.

But we talk about the Drake too. Both experiences were unforgettable, and one would not have been possible without the other.

No pain, no gain.

Chris Epting is the author of twenty travel/history books including *Roadside Baseball* and *The Birthplace Book*. He is also a journalist and travel writer, and he loves writing essays. Chris lives in Huntington Beach, California, with his wife and two children.

Natural Light

by SLOANE CROSLEY

I moved in when the vines were at their peak. I lived above the garden apartment in a brownstone, and up until that point most of the people I knew used their garden apartments for parties and patio furniture and, most egregiously, storage. If any of us had found it funny, we might have joked that the few weeds thriving between the concrete constituted "the garden." But we were too busy being thrilled by Chinese lanterns and outdoor grills to make that joke. My downstairs neighbor, Don, however, was not too busy. He meticulously kept the only actual garden I have ever seen in a Manhattan garden apartment.

I never knew Don's last name. He told me on the day I moved in as he shook my hand, but I have long since forgotten it. What I do know is that he was the thing more rare in New York City than a baby pigeon—a fantastic neighbor. After he introduced himself, he told me that if the vines around my bathroom window got too unruly, I should let him know. I didn't think much of this warning—how could a bunch of lush green and curling-to-the-point-of-flirty grapevines ever be considered unsightly? If anything I should thank him. But within a few weeks of moving in, the grapevines had almost completely obstructed the window, which I wouldn't have minded if that window wasn't responsible for half the apartment's natural light.

My fellow tenants and I casually referred to Don as the "self-appointed mayor" of our building. He did things like take in everyone's packages and keep track of the number of trash cans outside. He drove a vintage motorcycle, and his gray hair dripped down his back. The only times he ever irked me as a neighbor were the biannual all-day gardening fests in which he would blare the Grateful Dead for hours and at such a volume it ricocheted off the walls of the surrounding buildings like a siren's call to hippies everywhere. Not wanting to make Don get out the big ladder and the pruning sheers and climb all the way up to my window in his boxer shorts (once was enough), I would reach out the window as far as I could with kitchen scissors and hack at the vines. In the summer, I had to use a knife. Once the vines had been trimmed, I could see the myriad bushes and flowers and a water fountain down below. There was a single stone path, but every other surface was blanketed in moss and the roots of trees. When Don took notice of my trimming job, he told me that he hoped I enjoyed some of the grapes because he didn't know what to do with them.

I was resistant at first. Eating grapes that had come from Manhattan soil and rested on the same brick wall from which my air conditioner protruded? Oh, no thank you. When I finally got up the nerve to soak the Champagne grapes in my sink and consume them, I found them to be the best grapes I have ever tasted. (Maybe, I thought, grapes are better when they're hard won, only accessible via standing in my bathtub and reaching out the window.) Thus began phase two of my relationship with Don—the gifts.

I left him a bottle of wine to thank him for the fruit. I wanted to stay in-theme. He left me a bunch of tomatoes in return. One day I returned from work to find a package waiting outside my door with a note attached. I worked in book publishing, so I received a fair amount of books and manuscripts at home.

I'm guessing you could use this, said the note. *Hope this isn't too strange.*

Inside was a glossy photo book titled something like *Designing with Books.*

The next day I went to work and hunted down a copy of *Gardening in Small Spaces*. I left it outside his door with a trowel. Don was the only person I knew who could use it without hitting concrete. I had a side table outside of my apartment door with a cheap glass vase on it, and Don took to filling it with flowers from his garden on a weekly basis because it was "too depressing otherwise." When he learned that I'd written and sold a book of my own, he seemed legitimately concerned that I would be made uncomfortable by the flowers.

"In what world would flowers make me uncomfortable?"

"Well, now that you're famous, you probably get creepy things all the time."

"I don't think you understand how author fame works," I laughed.

One day, after a terrible day at work, I returned home to find a large single iris on my stoop. From a distance it looked like an abandoned pom-pom. I couldn't understand why the flower was outside and not in the vase, but I had a good hunch as to who had put it there. A note underneath read: *Our beloved neighbor Don of many years . . .*

I dropped my bag and reread those words maybe a dozen times. I still don't know who left the note and flower, but it's how I learned I was not Don's only friend in the building. This fact provided some vague comfort when I called my landlord the next morning and he told me Don had been dead for a week. He made a wrong turn on his motorcycle, drove into a bus on Second Avenue, and was in a coma for three days before he died. I never heard a single visitor in Don's apartment. I never heard him mention a member of his family or friend and never once ran into him on the street accompanied by anyone but himself. This dumb flower was the last symbol of Don as I knew him. I picked it up by the stem and sniffed, but, as Don could have told me, irises don't smell like anything.

The perfect tribute for my kind neighbor, to my mind, was to keep up the habit of putting flowers in the hallway vase. I did this for about three weeks and then stopped. They were expensive. Or, on a publishing salary, they felt like they were.

Plus I got lazy and distracted. The final straw was the realization that, because of the precise locale of my apartment—on the first floor and away from the main stairs—people rarely had cause to pass my door. All those garden flowers were only ever seen by me and the man who used to put them there.

Every spring, when it seems possible to have flowers and fresh things and fruit that has touched your air-conditioning unit but is still edible, I think of Don. I also think of how easily I gave up on my romantic tribute, although it was probably germane to a man whose last name I still don't know. Who really ever knows his neighbors well enough to leave them flowers to begin with?

The new tenants of Don's apartment moved in quickly afterward. They wanted a place to sit outside and read the paper in the morning, and so they uprooted most of Don's garden, including the vines. Which, if I'm honest with myself, wasn't so bad. I missed the garden, but I never had a problem with natural light again.

Sloane Crosley is the author of the *New York Times* bestselling books *How Did You Get This Number* and *I Was Told There'd Be Cake*, which was a finalist for the James Thurber Prize. Crosley is a frequent contributor to the *New York Times*, *GQ*, and National Public Radio (NPR). She writes, teaches, and lives in Manhattan in a neighborhood she thinks is the West Village but which the city of New York thinks is Chelsea.

Home Girl

by **APRIL SINCLAIR**

I have spent much of my adult life living alone, but ironically, I grew up in a house full of relatives. Once upon a time, I could seldom expect privacy. My sisters, Marcia and Nina, and I usually shared a comfortable bedroom, but at one point, there were five girls sleeping in our room. And for a minute, when I was a teenager, I even had to share my twin bed with a four-year-old niece. Nina says that one of her earliest memories is of me writing in the closet. I was probably just trying to find some solitude, trying to find my own private place. Not so easy with the ever-revolving cast of characters and relatives that called our brick bungalow their home.

Take "Aunt Shirley," who wasn't really my aunt at all, but a motherless girl who wasn't even a blood relative. My paternal grandmother took her in and raised her by herself. After Aunt Shirley got grown, she came and stayed with us for a while. Both of my grandmothers and one of my real aunts also lived under our roof at the time.

Aunt Shirley was known for her fish frying and wearing of miniskirts (which were in style), wigs, and a lot of makeup. Yet shapely Aunt Shirley was perhaps best known for receiving a lot of male attention. Half the time when the phone rang it was for her. Sometimes I felt like her secretary. I expressed surprise to my mother that Aunt Shirley had so many boyfriends calling when nobody would call her pretty. Mama told me that what made a woman popular wasn't always the brains or the beauty; sadly, it was often the booty.

One time, Aunt Shirley got a phone call from a man and my baby sister answered. Nina ran and told Aunt Shirley that Bill was on the phone. Aunt Shirley told Nina to tell Bill that she was asleep. My little sister went back to the telephone and said, "She says she's asleep." Aunt Shirley laughed as she took the receiver from Nina's hand.

Then there was Ray, my older half sister's husband. He knocked on our door one night and declared that he could no longer live with my sister, but had nowhere else to go. Sis had become pregnant and had their first daughter at age eighteen. Ray stood by her and married her. They went on to have two more children in a few years. My grandmother was keeping those kids at our house too. The girls shared a bed with Grandma after a brief stint in my bedroom. The baby boy was in a crib next to Grandma's bed. Ray and Sis shared a one-bedroom apartment and visited their kids at our house after work or on weekends. It was winter and my parents didn't want Ray to be homeless, so they allowed him to stay in our basement until he got on his feet. After two years, Ray met someone new and moved out with his daughters and remarried. Sis remarried also and kept their son with her and went on to have another son with her new husband.

Yep, there always seemed to be room for family in our home. I recalled seeing my uncle Sonny roll up in front of our South Side of Chicago home with his car packed with thirteen relatives and friends, every one of them excited about having taken a trip. Uncle Sonny had driven his five children and some family friends from Detroit to Chicago to visit us for the weekend. I did say, "thirteen." A couple of the friends stayed with their friends, and a few relatives were spread among other relatives. But that still left our house filled to the brim. We slept wall to wall, but us kids had a ball.

I'll never forget that steamy, summer evening when it was time for them to leave. The lightning bugs were out, flickering in the humid night air. All thirteen of them packed into the car for the long trip home, with me cramming the giggling youngest kid in like a sardine on top of two layers of laps. These were the days before mandatory seat belts, of course.

The accommodations during our highly anticipated, scrimped-and-saved-for trip to California weren't much different. When I was twelve, my mother, Aunt Jean, my three younger siblings, and I took the train all the way from Chicago to Los Angeles and stayed with a male cousin. Cousin Alfred had a one-bedroom apartment in L.A. My brother, Byron, slept in the living room with Cousin Alfred while my mother, aunt, and us three girls all slept in the one bed. Five people sleeping in one bed for a whole week! I used to dread nightfall. But somehow we made it through.

From L.A., our family took a day trip to Tijuana where I bought a straw sombrero for ninety-nine cents. When I returned to school in the fall, the other kids didn't believe that we'd been out to California, let alone Mexico, a foreign country. I wore my huge sombrero with "Made in Mexico" written on the front of it to school. I showed off pictures of us at Disneyland, and a photo of me holding up a gigantic fake boulder at Universal City Studios. Girls cut their eyes or sucked in their teeth, and sneered, "She thank she somethin'."

Suddenly, I felt out of place standing in that school hallway wearing my large sombrero. I felt alone. But back home, even though it was seldom quiet and I could get lost in a sea of relatives and visitors, I always knew who I was.

April Sinclair is the author of three novels, including the critically acclaimed bestseller *Coffee Will Make You Black*. Sinclair received the Carl Sandburg Award in Literature from The Friends of the Chicago Public Library. She has championed the cause of literacy in schools, juvenile halls, nonprofit organizations, adult prisons, and drug rehabilitation centers. April is a Chicago native who now resides in the San Francisco Bay Area.

Invisibility

by **MAILE MELOY**

Being invisible is complicated. It's possible, and the easiest way is if you have a bath of invisibility solution, which coats your skin and refracts light so no one can see you. People get excited when they hear that, because it seems like invisibility would make your life easier, or would allow you to get away with mischief. But it isn't that simple, and you don't realize all the inherent problems until you try it.

First, invisibility solution doesn't work on clothes. So you have to be naked to be invisible, or else you look like a ghost, or like a suit of empty clothes walking around—which is the opposite of invisibility, and just draws attention to whatever you're doing. Most of the things you want to do when you're invisible involve going outside, and it's cold outside with no clothes on, especially in winter. I don't know if you've tried that lately, but it's true.

If you're tough and brave, and don't mind being cold, then there's still another problem. If you become invisible with a friend, so you can have an adventure together, you won't be able to see each other. You can't make eye contact, which is part of the fun of having an adventure. And you're likely to bump into each other all the time, unless you leave one small part of your body visible so that you can see where your friend is. But it can't be an eye—it has to be a part of the body that no one else will notice: the tip of a nose, or half a finger, or a patch of knee. People aren't expecting to see a patch of knee floating along, so they don't see it. And even though you're looking for that patch, you might not notice it, either. So sharing the invisibility experience with someone else can be difficult, and you might just end up lonely.

The third problem is that invisibility solution wears off. And you can't predict, exactly, when and where it might wear off. You'll suddenly see your hand becoming visible, and then your forearm, and you'll realize it's starting to happen. You don't want to get caught naked out in the world, so you have to be ready to grab some clothes or a towel on short notice—though you can't carry the emergency covering with you, or it will look like a bundle of clothes floating in air. This problem isn't an impossible one, as long as you plan ahead. You just have to make your invisible adventures very short so you'll always get home before the stuff wears off.

Another thing people don't realize is that some of the things they want to do while invisible aren't actually very fun. Stealing is possible, but it just makes you feel bad, the same as it would if you stole while you were visible and just didn't get caught. So stealing isn't a good use of being invisible. Neither is hitting people who can't see you, or eating tons of free junk food you're not supposed to eat. Those just make you feel rotten and queasy afterward and you might start agreeing that the invisibility solution isn't so great.

But there is one alternate invisibility method, which I do recommend. There's no bath, and you don't become physically invisible, and you get to keep your clothes and your warm coat. It doesn't wear off until you want it to. You can't use it around your friends, because it usually doesn't work with them. But you can use it around strangers. You can't hit people or steal, but you can eavesdrop, which is the best part of being invisible anyway. When no one knows you're there, they say all kinds of things, and you can learn from what they say.

What you do is remain very still, and don't draw attention to yourself. Don't make eye contact with people—that's a dead giveaway that you're there. Don't say anything, or make noise, or walk in a way that makes people notice you. Make your footsteps quiet, and keep your arms and hands close to your body. Don't round your shoulders or hide or duck your head—that will make people wonder what's wrong with you. Just make yourself calm and still and ordinary. People will say things without thinking you're there, and they'll let you walk by without bothering you or asking you for anything. They won't notice anything you do.

Try it sometime. It's quicker than the invisibility bath, and warmer, and easier to control. It doesn't wear off unexpectedly, but you can shake it off whenever you want. Just look people in the eye, and smile, and make your movements bigger, and let your arms swing, and everyone will see you again.

Maile Meloy is the author of the novel *The Apothecary*, in which the characters learn to fly and to become invisible, and a new sequel, *The Apprentices*. She has also written two novels and two books of short stories for adults. She grew up in Helena, Montana, and now lives in Los Angeles.

The Most Famous Fairy-tale Cat of All Is a Furry-Faced Fabulist

by DAISY WHITNEY

Puss in Boots is a liar.

And yet, we still love him.

Because he's just sooo cute and he's got those boots. And let's face it—a cat wearing boots is cute. A talking cat is even better. And a talking, clever, helpful, and supportive cat? Sign me up, please.

I'm talking about Puss in Boots of fairy-tale lore here, and not just the *Shrek*-ified version. Though, let the record reflect, Puss in Boots is definitely my favorite character in that movie, for the same reason that he is my favorite fairy-tale creation too—he is dubious and complicated and much more than what meets the eye. He's neither black nor white, neither all good, nor all bad. He is the manifestation of moral ambiguity.

And even in spite of his bait-and-switch ways, Puss in Boots is a beloved character that both young and old are fond of. (Oh, what I wouldn't give for my cat to be more useful like Puss is!)

In the original French fairy tale by Charles Perrault, first penned in the seventeenth century, Puss in Boots is the gift that the miller's son receives upon his father's death. The son bemoans the feline bequeathment, complaining that one can't make money with a cat. Besides, the son laments, his two older brothers received better inheritances—a donkey and a mill, much finer ways to earn some dough. As it happens, the cat is no ordinary cat. Far slicker and faster than any mill or donkey, he's a veritable money-making machine. Puss is a con artist who can smooth talk his way in and out of any situation and connive money out of nearly anyone. Very quickly, the clever cat devises a strategy to turn his penniless owner into a man of great riches, the so-called Marquis of Carabas. Puss spins yarns to convince the king that the marquis is a rich and noble landowner deserving of the king's daughter's hand in marriage. And naturally, the miller's son and the king's daughter wed and live happily ever after, with their cat by their side.

So, is the lesson that deceit pays? That lying your way into marriage and wealth is admirable? After all, the cat, and by extension his owner, actively engage in trickery, deceit, and lies to win riches and a better position in life.

Or, perhaps there is another prism through which to view the cat. What if Puss is a Robin Hood, stealing from the rich to give to the poor so that the ends justify the means? By that same logic, is it then okay for Puss to lie out of loyalty to his owner? After all, the furry creature isn't lying for himself. He's simply a loyal servant.

I say Puss is both liar and servant. He is both sneaky and noble.

Sure, on the surface, he's a scam artist, the classic con man with loads of wit and personality. But he's also just a cat; thus, he comes wrapped in a package that's easy for young readers to relate to. He's the kind of animal kids want to pet and play with and have curl up in their laps. He's smart and he's devoted and he doesn't use his charms for himself. He uses them solely for the benefit of his master.

But yet, he is also a liar.

And as such, he is one of the first representations children encounter of a gray character in literature. He's not traditionally good, nor is he categorically bad. His actions reside in the fuzzy, muted middle. And so, *Puss in Boots* isn't a story with hard and fast morals, like the Star Wars movies, or books like *Harry Potter*, where good always trumps evil in the end.

Instead, Puss in Boots is one of the most ambiguous characters in children's storytelling. His morality isn't black or white, and I contend that is the point of the story. Puss helps us understand that there are people—and, at times, animals—who aren't all good and who aren't all bad. There isn't always a knight in shining armor, nor is there always a cold-hearted villain. Literature is full of complex characters who defy categorization, and Puss in Boots is one of the early characters that we meet as readers who fits that mold. And we meet him in a way that makes us feel comfortable with the lack of clarity.

We meet him as a cat.

And in that form, we are drawn to him—naturally. That's what makes it possible for readers to ask questions of themselves, such as: Is it okay to lie to gain status in life? When would such cons be acceptable and okay? At what point, if at all, are lines crossed by the cat's tricks? Is honesty always admirable?

Morally ambiguous characters help us gauge morals in the first place. We can put ourselves in their shoes—or boots—and ask how we would behave under similar circumstances.

Besides, isn't life full of morally ambiguous characters? We're sure to meet many people who don't fit the easy categorizations of other fairy-tale characters, such as Cinderella as good and the evil stepmother as bad. We're certain to encounter situations where we might behave more like Puss or more like his master than like a nobleman.

Perhaps the lesson, then, is that it's always best to have a cat do your dirty work—that is, if you can find a feline who's willing to work days. And if you do, I've got a few magic beans to give you in exchange for that cat.

Especially, if he comes outfitted in a good pair of boots.

Daisy Whitney is the author of *The Mockingbirds* and its sequel *The Rivals*. A graduate of Brown University, she lives in San Francisco, California, with her fabulous husband, fantastic kids, adorable dog, and two rather morally ambiguous cats. Her third novel, *When You Were Here*, will be released in 2013.

GRAPHIC ESSAY / PERSONAL ESSAY
Write (and /or draw) about a time when you felt like an outsider
and how you dealt with it.

On Facing My Fears

by KHALID BIRDSONG

WHEN I WAS ELEVEN YEARS OLD, I MOVED FROM ATLANTA, GEORGIA,
WHERE I LIVED WITH MY MOTHER AND YOUNGER SISTER,
TO HAMBURG, GERMANY, TO LIVE WITH MY FATHER, STEPMOTHER,
AND HALF SISTER. LEAVING EVERYTHING I KNEW BEHIND, AND
HAVING TO ADJUST TO A NEW COUNTRY, A NEW LANGUAGE,
AND A NEW SCHOOL WAS HARD. YET WHAT MADE IT EVEN
HARDER WAS LOOKING DIFFERENT FROM EVERYONE ELSE.
I HOPED THERE WOULD BE ONE MAGICAL MOMENT WHERE
EVERYTHING SNAPPED INTO PLACE AND I FELT LIKE I FIT IN...

THOUGH I WENT TO AN INTERNATIONAL SCHOOL, IT TURNED OUT
THAT I WAS THE ONLY AFRICAN-AMERICAN. THERE WERE KIDS IN
MY CLASS FROM COUNTRIES ALL OVER THE WORLD, BUT NO ONE
WHO LOOKED SIMILAR TO ME. I TRIED TO MAKE FRIENDS BY BEING
OPEN TO NEW PEOPLE AND SHOWING INTEREST IN THEM,
BUT I WAS SCARED. I DID MY BEST TO ACT CONFIDENT,
BUT UNDERNEATH, I BELIEVED THEY WERE JUDGING ME BY
THE COLOR OF MY SKIN.

THE CLASSES IN MY NEW SCHOOL WERE EXTREMELY DIFFICULT, AND I REALLY DIDN'T GET GOOD GRADES AT FIRST. I THOUGHT MY TEACHERS BELIEVED THAT ALL BLACK PEOPLE WERE SLOW OR STUPID. THERE WASN'T A REASON TO STUDY OR TO PUSH MYSELF IF NO ONE EXPECTED ME TO SUCCEED.

I TOLD MY FATHER THIS AND HE SAID THAT HE UNDERSTOOD MY STRUGGLES. HOWEVER, HE ALSO TOLD ME THAT RACE DOES NOT DETERMINE INTELLIGENCE, AND THAT I SHOULD COMMIT TO MY SCHOOLWORK AND SHOW THEM THAT I'M CAPABLE. AFTER MANY HOURS OF STUDYING AND STAYING FOCUSED ON MY GOAL, MY GRADES STARTED TO IMPROVE.

GERMAN WAS A REALLY CHALLENGING LANGUAGE
TO LEARN. AT FIRST I WAS SCARED TO TRY SPEAKING IT
BECAUSE I FEARED PEOPLE'S REACTIONS TO MY MISTAKES.
BUT MY DAD'S MESSAGE STUCK WITH ME...

* THANK YOU!

* WHAT IS THIS...

I REALIZED THAT THE ONLY WAY TO LEARN THE LANGUAGE
WAS TO TRY, FAIL, AND KEEP TRYING. EVEN THOUGH I WAS
FAR FROM FLUENT, I FORCED MYSELF TO HAVE AS MANY
CONVERSATIONS AS POSSIBLE.

*GOOD DAY!

MY TWO YEARS LIVING IN GERMANY REALLY HELPED ME TO GROW INTO A WISER YOUNG MAN. IT WAS A CHALLENGING TIME THAT PUSHED ME TO TRY HARDER AND TO THINK DEEPER.

I REALIZED, OVER TIME, THAT I SHOULDN'T MAKE ASSUMPTIONS ABOUT THE WAY OTHERS VIEW ME, AND MORE IMPORTANTLY, I SHOULDN'T LET THE STEREOTYPES THAT DO EXIST AFFECT THE WAY I VIEW MYSELF.

*GOOD MORNING

Khalid Birdsong is a cartoonist and a teaching artist living in California. He loves reading, traveling, and spending time with his family when he's not drawing. Khalid has published several comic books and draws a webcomic, *Fried Chicken and Sushi*, about his two years living in Japan.

Raised by Wolves

by SARAH PRINEAS

My sisters and I were raised by a wolf pack of wild women—by a wild mother who loved us (but had pretty much no idea how to raise us to be "normal") and by the bold, unruly female characters in the fictional stories we read. And yet, somehow, despite our corybantic upbringing—or maybe because of it—we all turned out okay.

Imagine first, if you will, a woman who has four children under the age of six years old, a woman who isn't all that excited about having kids in the first place. I think my mom went a little crazy for a while. She had so much energy—and such a need to escape—that she ran around the backyard until she wore down a rutted path in the grass. Around and around and around. Eventually she took that energy to the road, became a national record-setting distance runner, and collected an entire bookcase full of trophies.

While Mom was out crossing finish lines, my wolf-cub sisters and I were put in a fenced area in the backyard so we wouldn't stray into the busy road that went past our house. Kind of like a cage. Mom would just toss us out there and fling us a bunch of baloney sandwiches once in a while. Then she'd sprint off again. My dad was busy working a sixty- or seventy-hour-per-week job (so we had enough baloney sandwiches to eat), so he didn't participate much in raising the four wild animals that were his daughters.

I'm not saying my mother was a bad mother. She wasn't, not at all. She just wasn't like any other mother I've ever met.

I think my mom's wildness happened because she was a girl born at the wrong time. When she was a little kid, girls weren't supposed to be runners or car mechanics or scientists; they were expected to keep their dresses clean and their hair neatly combed. They were supposed to grow up, get married, and have kids of their own. When she was a kid, my mom wanted to play the saxophone, but the music teacher told her, "Girls don't play the saxophone." My mom should have been a saxophone-playing scuba-diving marine biologist. Instead she became a wild mom with wild daughters.

With our absent dad and running-away mom, we kids had to figure stuff out on our own. For example, you know how you're supposed to brush your teeth before you go to bed at night? I didn't figure that out until seventh grade. We wore hand-me-downs, not because we were poor, but because my mother hated to shop for clothes, and anyway, she wore raggedy jeans and T-shirts most of the time herself. During eighth grade, I wore the same plaid flannel shirt and holey jeans to school every single day. I loved that shirt. It was so soft. Haircuts were another thing. My mom did them for us, and we all looked like little boys with hair hacked short-short with blunt scissors. Our house was always an unbelievable mess because my mom was totally uninterested in doing housework. I never had friends over because the house was so embarrassing. My best friend lived all the way across town, and my mom wouldn't ever drive me to our play dates—so I had to bike over, six miles each way on a very busy, dangerous road. Without a bike helmet, of course.

Being raised by wolves like that meant I felt a little odd around kids being raised by actual humans. I felt odd because I *was* odd, and not always in a good way. Picture me in eighth grade: A scrawny girl with short, sticking-up hair and lopsided glasses and mossy teeth, wearing a ragged yellow flannel shirt and holey jeans. What a weirdo!

One thing that my mother did for us—a motherly thing, I mean—was take us to the public library once a week so we could stock up on books. It was there that I learned that even though I was raised by a wild mom, part of me could also be raised by *On the Banks of Plum Creek* and *The Secret Garden* and *A Wrinkle in Time*—books about wild girls just like me. The books helped me figure things out. Not things like teeth brushing and house cleaning, but the idea that being an odd, wild girl wasn't such a terrible thing. Take Laura Ingalls, for example. Just like me, Laura was one of four sisters. Remember how Laura sends her rival Nellie Oleson into the leeches in *On the Banks of Plum Creek*, and how Laura climbs into the flooded creek and almost drowns? Laura was wild. My sisters and I read those books and played being Laura and her older sister Mary and ran around wearing bath towels on our heads for our "long hair."

I read Frances Hodgson Burnett's *The Secret Garden* over and over again because it was about a wild girl, the bratty Mary Lennox. At first, Mary doesn't fit into her world, but she is stubborn, and she gets her dresses dirty, and she makes a place for herself. I fell in love with Madeleine L'Engle's *A Wrinkle in Time* because of awkward, smart, odd Meg Murry. Sometimes, just like Meg, I'd lie in my bed and listen to the "dark and stormy night" and wonder what the wind would bring me.

These other girls—Laura, Meg, Mary Lennox—they were girls living in strange places with weird families, but they all figured things out, eventually. Laura grows up and teaches school and marries Almanzo—and becomes a great writer. Meg uses her smarts and her recalcitrance to save her father's life, and later she becomes a scientist. Mary Lennox makes her place into a home and creates a beautiful garden.

And you know what? We all turned out okay. The fictional characters, my mom, and even me. It seems to me that even if we're weirdos or brats or troublemakers when we're kids, quite often we wild, odd, not-quite-fitting-in girls grow up to be something rather wonderful—strong, independent women.

Sarah Prineas lives in Iowa City, Iowa, and is the author of The Magic Thief series and the *Winterling* trilogy. She holds a PhD in English literature. Sarah is married and has two odd, wild children.

PERSUASIVE ESSAY

If you could steal one trait from an animal, what would it be and why?

Why We Need Tails

by NED VIZZINI

I confess that I have always wanted a tail for personal reasons. I have long dreamed of waking up in the morning and using my sleek, powerful tail to hit the snooze button on my alarm clock, so I could keep my hands comfortably stashed under my pillow. With a tail, I could write at my computer and drink tea at the same time without stopping my flow.

But I don't just want a tail for myself. All of humanity would benefit from having one.

Tails would help us in three important ways: by reducing traffic deaths, aiding small businesses, and encouraging reading.

First, let's clear up what sort of tails I'm talking about. Bunny tails, while cute, wouldn't add much to the human experience. In fact—and I know this is completely disgusting, but we can't mince words—a rabbit tail might make going to the bathroom more complicated. I envision a long, muscular tail with precise grasping ability—the tail of a New World monkey.

There are two types of monkeys: New World and Old World. Only the New World monkeys, from South America, possess prehensile tails. Among these, the spider monkey's is perhaps the most impressive. Spider monkeys are a little more than a foot high, but their tails are almost three feet long. They use them to swing through trees, pick things up, and hang from branches while they eat. (Using this strategy, they can eat large quantities of food in very short periods of time.)

So now let's talk about driving. America averages over thirty-seven thousand traffic fatalities per year. We can do better than that! No one likes putting his or her cell phone on speaker while driving. The police have attempted to stamp out driving and texting by issuing big fines, but these efforts have been disregarded. With a tail, a person could drive and talk on the phone at the same time and be much safer!

Secondly, tails would cause an explosion of small-business innovation in America and beyond. Like the Internet, human tails would require thousands of new products and services. Bath-product businesses could offer special shampoo and conditioner for tails. (Human tails would, of course, be hairy, so they wouldn't remind anyone of rat tails.) Packaging companies could come up with all sorts of boxes and containers, custom-designed to be opened by tails. The cosmetic and apparel industries would explode. The options for accenting tails are endless. People could get tail piercings. The jewelry would be nuts! People could buy jeans that properly emphasized their tails with slick holes. They could dye their tails. They could curl them, straighten them, or have them adjusted to certain lengths.

But the most amazing options for tails are ones I can't conceive of. It would be up to the creative business innovators of the world to properly utilize this new part of human anatomy. Can you think of a good product to market to tail enthusiasts?

My final argument for tails is that they would let people read much more frequently. Reading while walking is difficult, but with a long enough tail you could hold the book or e-reader in an arc over your head and keep both hands free. Tails would also make reading in bed much more comfortable (and easier to do without your parents knowing). On a subway or bus, reading with your tail would give other people a chance to see all your hip tail accessories. The human tail would cause a spike in literacy rates across the board.

It's hard to believe, but some people think that tails would actually be detrimental to society. Their main argument is that a tail would make society fatter and contribute to obesity, allowing people to do fifty percent more while sitting down. However, having one might be so fun that it would encourage more people to exercise! And the children of the world would have exponentially more joy on the "monkey" bars. I'm confident that tails would make people healthier overall.

The good news is we may be closer to having tails than one might think. The human embryo actually develops a tail one-sixth the size of its body that gets absorbed as the embryo develops. Sometimes it doesn't quite disappear, and a person is born with a vestigial tail. The longest on record measured nine inches. Perhaps in the future these embryotic tails will evolve into the type that I imagine.

In so many ways, the human race has lost the ability to dream. But there's no reason to give up hope. There are a lot of "tall tails" out there, but this idea isn't one of them. If and when we do manage to grow tails, we'll certainly see the world change for the better. I, for one, am ready. Now, go get me my tail!

Ned Vizzini is the author of *The Other Normals*, *It's Kind of a Funny Story*, *Be More Chill*, and *Teen Angst? Naaah. . . .* He has written for the *New York Times*, The Daily Beast, and season 2 of MTV's *Teen Wolf*. His work has been translated into seven languages. He is the co-author, with Chris Columbus, of the forthcoming fantasy-adventure series House of Secrets. Ned lives in Los Angeles with his wife and son.

Death Is Only a Horizon

by ALANE FERGUSON

I've been asked many times why my novels consistently revolve around the topic of death, from autopsies to exploring the world of the paranormal. The answer to that question is as simple as it is complex because it is rooted in the tragic loss of my best friend at the hands of a serial killer. Her murder left a mark upon my soul, a spiritual scar covering a wound that will never completely heal. It hasn't been all sadness, though, because, in truth, her passing set me on a spiritual journey that has been long, winding, and ultimately cathartic. Some days I feel buoyed by a presence that wraps itself around me like a cool breeze. Other moments I think I catch a glimpse of my friend Savannah in a watery reflection, or wonder if I hear her whisper through the shadows of my dreams. In the end, I've discovered she has never been far from me. And so I write as a way to connect back to her. I create mysteries where she lives instead of dies, and justice always prevails.

If only real life were so easy.

A bit of background: Savannah Anderson was an only child murdered on Mother's Day when she was twenty-three and I was twenty-two. If I close my eyes, I can still hear the anxiety in her voice when we shared our last phone call—she made me promise to talk to her that weekend because she had something important to tell me about her new boyfriend. It pains me to confess that I blew that call off, confident that we could catch up another day. Here's a truth I've discovered about life: When death knocks, there is no "later." Kneeling at her grave, the scent of her funeral flowers wafting in the air, I was confronted with the hardest question anyone can face, and that is, What really happens when we die?

My father is an aerospace engineer, and so it makes sense that I began to look into the afterlife through the lens of science. I studied the mechanics of mortality and, in my early writings, explored graveyards and strange poisons that mimicked death. Further research took me to actual autopsies, where I witnessed human remains taken apart as if they were pieces of a puzzle, each portion meticulously inspected for secrets that might be revealed.

I remember leaning in to watch, fascinated, as the forensic team opened up body after body. One day, I was asked to weigh a man's brain, and before I knew it, that human organ was placed in my gloved fingers. I couldn't help but gasp, marveling that every thought of that man's life had been processed through this deceptively heavy, creased, gray matter. And I wondered—was this the essence of the man himself? A blob of tissue? As I dutifully weighed the brain, I realized that I finally had my answer. There had to be more to humanity than this clump of human cells. The deceased human body is called "remains" for a reason, because that is all that remains when the life energy departs. But *where* does that energy go? What happens to the human soul? Probing a cadaver with bloody forceps could not give me the explanations I craved, which led me to a very different kind of research: paranormal investigation.

Paranormal exploration (the study of supernatural occurrences that can't be explained by ordinary science) delves into the flip side of humanity's coin, where one travels from the physical into the mystical. I have to admit I was nervous to step beyond the certainty of science into this galaxy-sized unknown, but if Savannah were somehow within reach, I knew I had to try to find her. And so a new chapter began. With a vow to not let my imagination—or fear—get the best of me (I do all of my ghost hunting at night.), I crept though ancient cemeteries, Irish castles, and old buildings. I even walked side by side with Syfy Channel's *Ghost Hunter* team in a search for lost souls. And some eerie things did occur. Doors inexplicably opened. Objects moved. I've taken pictures with my own camera that seem to defy explanation, some revealing a swirling mist in an empty room, while others glowed with orbs of light that contained images of human faces. Yet, during these "hunts," I realized I was afraid to conjure the one person whose presence I'd craved the most: Savannah.

Here's another truth I've discovered about life: Sometimes you have to dig deep.

Countless books put forth the idea that a human soul violently jerked out of his or her body may be too disoriented to fully leave loved ones behind, and thus they remain earthbound. The idea unsettled me. Might this be the fate of my best friend? Her death was so brutal, so senseless. Finally I understood that this idea of her soul being mercilessly trapped in the in-between was the crux of what truly haunted me.

I grappled with my fears until, at last, the answers were revealed. The message was delivered to me as I stood atop St. Augustine's Lighthouse, a historical landmark purportedly rife with spirits. I remember leaning over the metal railing, lost in thought as the ocean broke against the shore. As always during a ghost hunt, Savannah's image was in the forefront of my mind. I was thinking about her when I distinctly heard the faraway notes of a Carly Simon song wafting somewhere below. "Life is eternal / and love is immortal / and death is only a horizon." How strange that I, a Colorado girl, would hear those words while staring into the sea. To me, the song was a message from my friend. I believe she was telling me that our souls never die; although her story had been cut short, her own pages were still unfolding in eternity because love is immortal. I could feel a kind of letting go. It was almost as if she had whispered she would help me live my life for both of us because she'd been with me all along.

I continue to use writing as a conduit to face what I don't fully understand, carefully painting the facts as I imagine them. On the forensic pages, I create a world where Savannah still lives, where I make a phone call before it is too late. In my paranormal stories, Savannah Anderson (the name of my protagonist) comes to grips with her own violent, untimely death while she learns to guide those left behind. I circle back to this topic of mortality because my stories allow me, the author, to introduce readers to my friend, an incredible and now immortal soul.

Alane Ferguson is the author of the Forensic Mysteries series, the Edgar Award–winning *Show Me the Evidence,* and many other novels and mysteries. For her forensic mysteries, Alane does intensive research, including interviewing forensic pathologists and attending autopsies. She lives in Colorado.

PERSONAL ESSAY

Is the grass always greener? Write about a time when someone else's circumstances or belongings seemed more appealing than your own.

Blue Jeans, Cat Stevens, and My First Kiss

by LISE CLAVEL

I've never had a pair of jeans I liked. It seems the styles change often enough that at some point what's in fashion should also fit me—I have two legs of pretty much the same length, hips wider than my waist, and no abnormal protuberances—but I've spent years looking for the perfect pair. It seems to go more easily for others, and a lot of my sense of what looks good has come from pining after the perfectly faded knees of someone else's jeans. I now realize that much of what I wanted as a young girl—the right clothes, the right relationships with boys—was defined by what I saw in other people. It took me some time to figure out that no one else's jeans would fit me exactly right, that I had to find my own.

In sixth grade, I saved up my allowance to buy a pair of Levi's that fit the way my classmates' did: tight. I probably bought the same size my friends were wearing, which made them maybe just a bit tighter on me. Or it could have been that my mom washed them wrong, or that I pulled them up too high, or that I'd bought a different style than everyone else.

The only day I ever wore them, I arrived at school with a relief tinged with nervousness: relief because I finally had the right jeans, nervousness that someone would notice how not-quite-right they were. And, of course, someone did. It was Elizabeth B., who showed off a new pair of trend-setting shoes every Monday morning on the bus, who had brand-name everything and a strange power over the rest of us, the same girl who, in seventh grade, didn't just have a boy she was "going out with," but rather an actual boyfriend. Most of us wouldn't make that scary yet alluring upgrade till high school.

Elizabeth looked me up and down and said, "Nice leggings."

Now leggings may be cool in the twenty-first century, but in 1992 they definitely weren't. With those two words, Elizabeth had made it clear that I'd failed. At the time, my understanding of that failure was that I'd bought the wrong jeans and if only I could find the right pair, all would be well. Elizabeth's jeans looked great to me—but did she think so? Other people's lives seem more exciting than our own.

I'll never forget, for instance, standing outside a museum at age ten, watching a European couple kissing for minutes on end. That cinematic image of foreign people engaged in a foreign act was burned on my mind for years. I wanted *that*.

My first kiss. Those words encompassed a lot for a long time. What would it be like? Who would it be with? Would it happen to me too long after it did to everyone else, like losing my baby teeth had? When I finally got to the answers—1. nothing momentous 2. Jamie D. 3. sort of, but not really—the entire idea of the event, which I'd been imagining for years, deflated quite quickly. It wasn't bad, and it wasn't good; but either way, it certainly didn't fill in the colors my imagination had prepared for the painting. Rather, reality struck.

Jamie and I were both in eighth grade. He went to an all-boys' school. I went to an all girls' school. Maybe we danced once together at some kind of event whose awkwardness seemed reserved for kids in junior high (but, as it turns out, awkwardness pretty much defines all social "mixers," no matter the age level. I stick as close to the pretzel bowl now as I did then; if I am to be afflicted with small talk, I at least deserve some dietary sustenance). Maybe my friend Jane or Rebecca set us up. I can't remember. In either case, I know Jamie and I talked on the phone every night, and that I worked diligently to bring some interesting topics to the table. What kinds of movies do you like? Can you believe what my science teacher said today?—that sort of thing. I knew his phone number by heart. That was a prerequisite for going out with a boy, for sure. I won't say whether I still have his number memorized.

We kissed for the first time on a Saturday afternoon. Somehow we were in his bedroom, categorically against my mother's rules, and his parents weren't home. I wore jeans, of course, according to the eternal rule of "look nice but casual on a date," and a long-sleeved green shirt from Banana Republic that I'd gotten as a gift for church Confirmation earlier that year. Jamie and I were talking in that stilted way two people talk when they know something's about to happen, and they want to make sure it happens but also know that, at all costs, the thing cannot be spoken of or even alluded to. It may be reserved for first kisses, the mentality of: We are trying very hard to get to this place but under no circumstances will we discuss how to achieve our goal or even glance in such a direction. In fact, we will in all cases act as if we've got hundreds of more important things on our minds.

He was telling me about his CD-ROM, which was at the time a new technology. I still had a tape deck, so the idea of playing a CD through the computer was astonishing. It seemed the sort of thing I'd just never have, no matter how popular it got, a little like something neat you see advertised in an infomercial. He played the songs "Oh, Very Young" and "Father and Son," both lovely Cat Stevens songs, through his desktop. I hadn't heard those songs before.

I was half-sitting, half-lounging on his bed, half-embarrassed and terrified and nervous all at the same time, when he kissed me. It lasted for a minute or two. He moved his tongue around in my mouth, and his breath was neither bad nor appealing. Probably someone's arm was caught somewhere uncomfortable, behind a neck or holding up half a body, but if that was the case neither of us did a thing to change it. I was trying to hold on to what kissing felt like so I could wonder about it later. This was difficult, though, since I was simultaneously thinking, "We're kissing! I've never French-kissed before!" and imagining how I would retell the event to my best friends.

But kissing Jamie does not stick in my memory as something momentous. Nor did it at the time. The novelty ended when I left his apartment. I spent more time running my tongue along my front teeth a few months later, marveling at the slimy smoothness right after I got my braces taken off, than I did playing back the kiss with Jamie. You might be wondering, then, why I bother retelling the moment.

It's precisely because it means nothing to me, because the moment was perfectly unromantic, because I had spent years fantasizing about my first kiss and the actual event could not have felt less cinematic or stripped of intrigue.

Things don't happen like they do in the movies or in your dreams or, as seemed most important in junior high, the way they happen to everybody else. I was jealous of Elizabeth's clothes and shoes and seemingly easy-to-come-by experience with boys, but I don't know how any of those things felt to her. Her life was just part of my imagination—more vivid and tangible, in a way, than my own coming-of-age experience. And it took a long time to realize that imagination can be the experience, that it is often richer and more inspiring than whatever reality it gestures toward.

I'm still looking for a good pair of jeans as well as learning to walk past the movie theaters of other people's lives.

Lise Clavel was the Virginia State Director for "Obama for America" in 2012. Before getting into politics, Lise was a teacher at the Mountain School of Milton Academy in Vermont. She holds a BA from Yale University, where she won the thesis prize for her work on the poet John Ashbery.

LITERARY ESSAY

What is your favorite story? Explain what makes this story so compelling.

King Arthur's Great Power

by **MARY-ANN OCHOTA**

From parables in the Bible, to blockbuster movies, to the tall tales and gossip of the schoolyard, we instinctively know when we come across a good story: One that grips us, where we care about the characters and can't wait to discover what happens next. One where we hang on every word issuing from the storyteller's mouth. One where we physically feel the power of the tale unfolding before us.

Only humans have the capacity to create such rich imaginary worlds. Only *Homo sapiens* have the ability to empathize with imaginary people, and genuinely be moved by their adventures. From our first cave art depictions, we have used narratives to relay our past, understand our present, and shape our future.

One of the most compelling legends, a story that has stayed exciting and relevant for almost a thousand years, is the story of King Arthur.

Arthur, it is said, became king of the Britons when he pulled the famous sword Excalibur from the stone in which it was magically trapped. He became an extraordinary leader, presiding over a court of courageous warriors called the Knights of the Round Table. With Arthur as king, brave deeds were rewarded, the poor and the weak were protected, good triumphed over evil. In these tales, the vivid characters that surround Arthur enrich the stories, giving them color even to modern ears—his best friend, the knight Lancelot; his trusted adviser, the wizard Merlin; his beautiful wife, Guinevere. And Arthur also has the protection of powerful magic—including the enchanted sword that started it all.

The first tales of Arthur were written in the 1130s by a monk named Geoffrey of Monmouth, who was asked to write a history of the kings of Britain. Those who supported him were wealthy French noblemen who had invaded Britain less than a century before, and who were still fighting off rebellions by the local people. These French rulers wanted Geoffrey to write an account of British history that traced a direct line of royal succession from the heroic King Arthur to them . . . even if it wasn't quite true. Through the power of Arthur's story, the French nobility were encouraging people to believe that the French had a genuine right to rule England, and that by invading Britain they were just reclaiming what was rightfully theirs to begin with.

The tale of King Arthur was quickly picked up by poets, singers, painters, and writers, who elaborated and extended it. As the story grew in prominence, kings began to use it, not just to validate their rule, but also as a way to impress others. King Edward I used to eat his dinner at a round table, and when important guests would visit, he would show them what he claimed was the true Excalibur. King Henry VIII, too, had his portrait painted on what, at the time, was thought to be the real Round Table, along with the names of such famous knights as Sir Lancelot, Sir Gawain, and Sir Tristram. There are even pictures of King Arthur in the modern-day British Houses of Parliament! Clearly Arthur is a powerful friend to have.

But have we all been celebrating a fictitious character, or did King Arthur ever really exist?

If there ever was a real Arthur, chronicles from the Middle Ages suggest that he would have lived in Britain in the fifth or sixth century—more than fifteen hundred years ago. It's a time known as the Dark Ages because the ancient Romans left and the native Britons seemed to have gone back to an earlier, less sophisticated lifestyle. No more plush Roman villas—instead, round houses, defensive hill forts, and smaller, tribal kingdoms. And crucially, few of their written records survive.

None of the very early British writers mention anyone named Arthur. The earliest mentions, from around the year 800, suggest that right from the outset, Arthur was a legendary warrior rather than a real one—unless a person can really kill 940 soldiers on his own in one afternoon on a battlefield in Wales.

What's clear is that the power of Arthur's story doesn't fade as time passes. Many people nowadays search for Arthur's last resting place, for the Holy Grail, for the lost sword

Excalibur . . . and many believe he's going to come back and save us from the next lot of bad guys, whoever they are.

The story of King Arthur has danger, excitement, love, and adventure. What our ancestors wanted from a story is exactly what we want. So next time Hollywood creates a new King Arthur and you sit back with a bucket of popcorn to enjoy it, you can feel part of an ancient lineage that includes those who have used the King Arthur story to strengthen their political position and those who have simply enjoyed it as one of the greatest stories in history.

Mary-Ann Ochota is an anthropologist and TV host. She completed her degree in anthropology and archaeology at Cambridge University. Mary-Ann has made TV shows about British archaeology, weird human habits, feral children, and Roman bread. She's completed research on subjects including Christmas, what we mean when we say we're "healthy," and how new technologies change how we think. When she can, Mary-Ann heads out of London to go sailing, hiking, horseback riding, and scuba diving. When she's in London she hangs out with her family, her friends, and her dog, Harpo.

A Thousand Truths: (Mostly) a Good Dog

by STEVE BREZENOFF

There is an old saying: "One lie ruins a thousand truths." But after a lifetime of living honestly, can one mistake really undo all the good you've done? Harry doesn't think so. He's been a loving, gentle, and good dog for nearly ten years. Today, though, there is a single scar on his history, and also on a little boy's cheek.

No one knows how Harry ended up on the rough streets of Brooklyn, New York—at least, no one who can speak—and no one can say how he managed to survive those harsh conditions. He was skinny—only fourteen pounds—with a festering rat bite in his belly when he was found one day in June and taken to the Brooklyn Animal Care Center. By the time he was one year old, though, the tough little terrier had proven just how tough he was.

But he wasn't just tough; he was also cute and smart. He stayed only two weeks at the center before his online profile— with a photo of Harry, leashed to a big, rough-looking hand— attracted adopters. They liked his long-haired little snout, his white and tan—almost orange—coat, and his brown and mournful eyes. When they came to get him, he scrambled out of the back room, onto the cold tile floor of the center's lobby, and peed. It was no little pee, either. It was a torrential pud-dling of bright yellow urine. That meant, of course, that Harry already knew he shouldn't pee in his pen, a clear indication that Harry was (nearly) housetrained.

Once at his new home, Harry got right to settling in. It was a hot summer in Brooklyn, and Harry found the coolest spot to lie down—a slab of marble between the kitchen and living room. At night, he slept in the big chair next to his new own-ers' bed, way up high where he could see them, watch them, and keep them safe.

Harry lived in Brooklyn for the first few years of his life—initially on his own, and then with his new family. One day in the spring of 2006, though, he hopped into the car and sat on a lap for nearly two days straight: He was moving to Minne-sota. After a life of sidewalks and pavement and concrete lots, Harry was hitting the country.

Only a block from his new apartment, Harry found a huge dog park, replete with waterfalls and trails through the woods and the biggest body of water he'd ever seen: the Mississippi River. Harry charged the water; he didn't jump in, though—terriers aren't water dogs, after all. He snapped at the little waves and barked at the rolling river. He'd never had so much fun, and he settled into life in Minnesota as quickly as he had into his Brooklyn apartment.

Over time, Harry had become a great cuddler. He spent hours on the couch with one or both of his humans, while they read or watched TV or typed on the computers on their laps. At night, Harry was allowed right into bed with them. He'd often sleep among their feet, but on the colder winter nights, he crawled right between them, like a hot water bottle with legs and fur. Life was pretty great.

One day at the end of an easy summer, the humans brought home the funniest little thing: a tiny, smelly person. Harry investigated, but there wasn't much to see. It hardly moved. It couldn't talk. Eventually it started dropping spoons covered in delicious things. Harry liked that.

The new baby wasn't the first kid Harry had seen. On walks over the years, he'd been harassed by little hands and funny little faces. One boy in the neighborhood even tried to climb onto his back, as if Harry were a little horse, perfectly sized for toddlers. Harry didn't growl or bark or snap at these kids, not even the would-be cowboy. He put up with it. He proved himself patient and gentle, over and over.

He did the same with the new boy in his house, who grew like a weed. The boy went from crawling and crying to walking and screaming to running and grabbing. At times, the boy went too far, like the wild kids in the street. The boy patted Harry, trying to do it right, but just a little too rough, a little too hard. Harry remained patient.

The boy liked to build forts. He liked to use every pillow in the house and every blanket he could find, even the ones Harry liked to nap on. The boy tugged and tugged at those blankets and pillows, and Harry snarled a warning: *Leave my pillows and blankets alone, newbie.* But the boy pulled and pushed too much, and a lifetime of truths was placed in jeopardy. Harry reared up and snapped, and he caught the boy on the apple of his cheek.

There was a little bit of blood and a lot of tears. The tears lasted longer for the big humans. Though it was an easy decision to make, it was a hard decision to carry out. Harry had to go. After so many happy years full of affection and cuddling, the risk of keeping Harry was too great; the humans needed to make sure the boy would always be safe. Since Harry had never been formally trained, they considered sending him to obedience school. But there was still no guarantee that it wouldn't happen again, and maybe next time Harry would take off a lip or a piece of ear.

They resigned themselves to Harry's fate and found a new home for him—a house with one other dog and just one human, a full-grown one. In Harry's new house, his playmate is another terrier, a few pounds heavier and a few inches longer, with a blotch of black where Harry's blotch is that nearly orange tan. They're a great pair.

Harry made one great mistake, and everyone had to deal with the consequences. But with so many memories and so many years of being such a good boy, is it true that "one lie ruins a thousand truths"? Harry doesn't think so, and neither do we.

Steve Brezenoff wrote *The Absolute Value of −1* and *Brooklyn, Burning*, as well as dozens of chapter books for young readers. Though Steve grew up in a suburb on Long Island, he now lives with his wife and son in Minneapolis, Minnesota.

Death by Host Family

by **CASEY SCIESZKA** and **STEVEN WEINBERG**

We are going to die. We are going to die on this crazy motor-cycle contraption in the middle of the Colombian jungle and our moms are going to be *so mad*.

How did we get into this mess? For the past few weeks, Steven and I have been backpacking through the South American country of Colombia, learning Spanish, taking butt-breaking bus rides, and making friends.

We stopped in the city of Cali for a few days and met a man named Mauro at a corner store where we were buying water. No, we don't usually make friends with strangers on the street, but in our five years of traveling and living abroad together, Steven and I have found that sometimes when you're in a foreign place, new friends turn up in odd places. And it's always worth making new friends in new places because they are the ones who can show you the *real* side of their country, not just what every regular old tourist sees.

Mauro was an artist—a ceramicist—so he was *really* excited when we told him Steven was an artist too. Next thing we knew, we were staying in his house with his wife Diyana and their three children, and then were on our way to a family vacation with them in the jungle! Just like that, they became our Colombian host family.

Let me pause here for a moment to say, we love host families. For a lot of our travels—from Morocco to China to even Timbuktu—we have made friends with or even lived with families that then became our home away from home. Host families are great for a million reasons. For example, we get to eat amazing and authentic home cooking, we're usually on the same language level as the youngest kid in the family so we have an automatic best friend, and we can have all the local customs that we don't understand explained to us.

Sometimes, though, host families can be confusing. For example, maybe what your host family is doing isn't a local custom at all. Maybe it's just totally *crazy* and you're mistaking one individual's insanity for the whole country's culture—which leads us to where we are right now. Would a *normal* Colombian family take a vacation to a place where the only way to get around is by riding this crazy contraption? Or is our new host family *nuts*?

During our three-hour car ride from the city of Cali to the jungle, Diyana explained that these devices we were about to get on were called *brujas* (sounds like "broohas") and that they work like this:

MOTORCYCLE

PLANK OF WOOD

BEARINGS

OLD RAILROAD
NO LONGER
IN USE

TWO BENCHES

AS MANY PEOPLE
YOU CAN FIT

How do they stop? Not so well. What do you do when another one is coming from the opposite direction? Panic. More specifically, haul your *bruja* off the tracks before the oncoming one can hit you.

All that said, after a few harrowing minutes, I have to admit . . . this is REALLY fun. We're whipping along, the jungle wind is blowing our hair back, and we're squealing as we cross bridges and fly around blind corners. The countryside is zipping by and we are going so FAST.

By the time we get off the *bruja* twenty minutes later, we've all got on huge grins (and probably bugs in our teeth), and I'm secretly disappointed that the ride is finished so quickly even though it almost killed us. This family may be kind of nutty for taking us on a contraption like this—and maybe we're kind of nutty for going along with it—but man, do they know how to have a good time! We can only imagine what's next.

That's when Mauro says, "There is this very, very old and very, very high rope swing hanging over the river . . ."

Casey Scieszka wrote and *Steven Weinberg* illustrated *To Timbuktu*, which tells the story of their first two years out of college spent living in Asia and West Africa. Casey and Steven are from Brooklyn and Washington, D.C., respectively. They've set up camp all over the world—from China to Mali to Morocco—but are currently Brooklynites.

The Incredibly Amazing Humpback Anglerfish

by **MICHAEL HEARST**

As you may or may not know, many unusual creatures live in the deep, dark ocean. Carnivorous giant squid with tentacles reaching up to sixty feet in length swim across the continental slope. Scotoplanes crawl along the abyssal plane like tiny piglets scavenging for debris. And ferocious-looking, deep-sea fish with long growths protruding from their heads, lit up at the ends like flashlights, lurk within the frigid darkness. This third creature that I speak of is the humpback anglerfish. I am particularly fascinated by this creature, not only because it is *so* unusual looking, but also because of the way in which it benefits from these amazing and peculiar features.

Whenever someone sees a humpback anglerfish (or a picture of one, more likely), a common question arises: Why does it have a light rod sticking out from its forehead? The answer can be found in the name itself: anglerfish. The word *angler* refers to one who fishes with a lure. And just like a fisherman, the female humpback anglerfish uses its fishing pole to attract prey. The luminescent bacteria at the end of the growth glows in the dark, acting as a lure to attract other fish to swim within reach (much like how a light bulb attracts a moth). And then, with a quick snap, the anglerfish lurches forward, devouring its victim whole. The bones of the humpback anglerfish are thin and flexible, allowing the body to stretch, and enabling this fish to eat prey twice its own size!

In addition to this peculiar method of hunting for food, the humpback anglerfish has another intriguing trait, and that is the manner in which it procreates. What I'm about to tell you might sound made up (Actually, the bit about the light pole sticking out of its head also sounds made up.); however, it's all true. While the female humpback anglerfish measures only about four inches in length, the male is even smaller, about forty times smaller! This little guy exists with the sole purpose of finding a female. Upon encounter, the tiny male anglerfish bites into the skin of the larger female, and a reaction takes place: The male's body begins to fuse into hers. Even their blood vessels join together. Ultimately, the male anglerfish dissolves almost entirely into the body of the female, becoming just a lump on her skin. The remaining lump of what was once the male anglerfish stays attached, ready to fertilize her eggs when the time comes. How's that for unusual?

But why, you may ask, do I personally care to research such a strange fish? I'll tell you why: because I love unusual things. Not just deep-sea creatures, but also unusual people, unusual toys, unusual musical instruments, and just about anything else unusual that you can think of. The truth is I get bored with common things. I prefer theremins to guitars, wind-up automatons to LEGOS, and, you guessed it, animals like the humpback anglerfish to horses. Come to think of it, the very fact that I'm interested in so many unusual things makes me even more unusual. Perhaps I'm more similar to the humpback anglerfish than I thought. And to my delight, I get to spend my days writing about such strange animals and other quirky things, as well as composing music that sounds quite different from what you typically hear. In my opinion, there are enough books about cats and dogs, and way too many songs played on the guitar.

We all have our unique angles in life. We all adapt in our own way. And if we look below the surface, in the vast under-explored sea of unusual creatures, the humpback anglerfish might just teach us a thing or two, that being different may actually have its advantages.

Michael Hearst is a composer, multi-instrumentalist, and writer. He is a founding member of the band One Ring Zero, which has released nine albums. Michael's solo works include the albums

Songs for Ice Cream Trucks and *Songs for Unusual Creatures*, as well as the soundtracks for the movies *Magic Camp, The House of Suh,* and *The Good Mother.* Michael has toured with The Magnetic Fields, performed with The Kronos Quartet at Carnegie Hall, and appeared on such shows as NPR's *Fresh Air,* A&E's *Breakfast with the Arts,* and NBC's *Today Show.* As a writer, Michael is the author of the book *Unusual Creatures.* His work has also appeared in such journals as *McSweeney's, The Lifted Brow,* and *Post Road.*

Showering with Spiders

by CLAY McLEOD CHAPMAN

Taking a shower in a coffin. That's exactly what it felt like. We're talking wooden floorboards, where the water trickles through the cracks just beneath your feet. A wooden door—hinged with a coil of rusted wire that springs shut as quickly as you opened it, squealing as it seals you inside. Count 'em—four wooden walls, warped boards gone gray from all those years of salty ocean air.

And spiders. Hidden behind the shower head. Perched upon the water knobs. Tucked between the floorboards just below your toes.

When I was about five years old, my family packed up the car and headed off to the beach for a week-long sunburn. We stayed in a ramshackle summer cottage with a chunk of beach that we called all our own, swimming the week away.

House rule numero uno: No sand inside.

The outdoor shower was tucked underneath our cottage's back deck. Half the nails holding it together had rusted into an orange paste. The knots in the wood looked like the eyes of an elephant, all gray. I almost expected them to blink back at me. I was so small that the shower head towered overhead, looking more like a metal sunflower pulled free of all its petals, drooping on its stem. When I turned on the water, the stream branched out from the spigot like a spider web falling over my shoulders.

Then I looked up—wait up. Hold on a sec.

There was a web. A web-behind-the-web. Tucked just behind the shower head was a netting of silk. A spider's web. It just barely billowed in the breeze, as if the temperature had dropped fast enough for the shower to freeze in mid-spritz. Some stray drops of water clung to the web, trapped along with what appeared to be two rotting flies.

But where was the spider?

Cautious cleaning. That's what I did. I kept my eyes open for that spider, wherever it might be, washing up as fast as humanly possible. Legs? Check. Armpits? Check. Tummy? Check.

No spider.

Next came washing my face. I actually had to close my eyes. That soap was so old, it was practically petrified. Water was no good at getting it to suds up. It felt like I was washing with a rock.

A dollop of soap dribbled into my eyes. I instantly winced. I balled up my fists and started rubbing, determined to knuckle the soap out of my eyes before it burned my retinas away.

We're talking seven seconds of blindness. Ten at most.

I blinked back into focus. Only to feel something on my

shoulder. Something heavier than water. Just a millionth of a milligram more. I turned my head, slowly.

There it was: Yellow stripes. Eight legs. A bulb of a belly as fat as a blueberry.

And it was crawling toward my chin.

I froze. My heart shriveled into itself like the dried husk of one of the flies caught in the web above my head. And I peed. That's right—you heard me: I peed. In my swimming trunks. Because there I was, sealed inside some wooden box that might as well be a coffin, my coffin, staring down eight different eyes staring right back at me—and for the moment, I was paralyzed. I couldn't move. I couldn't scream. I couldn't even breathe. All I could do was watch it crawl closer toward my chin, feeling the slight pinch of its legs against my skin, those yellow stripes running down its back slowly unraveling from around its body and weaving about my brain, wrapping so tightly around my memory forever, like a bow on a present I'd never ever want to open. Saying a prayer at this point would have been too much like my last rites—I wanted out of this pine box, not to be buried in it.

It's hard to remember what kind of defensive maneuver came next. My knees must have softened, sending my shoulder under the flow of water. The spider instantly curled up into a clump of wet limbs and washed away, looking like a tiny tumbleweed rolling over the floorboards before slipping through the cracks between my feet. I stood there under the running water for I don't know how long. Long enough to prune up.

Long enough to know that that spider wasn't going to come crawling back.

I refused to step inside that shower for the rest of the week.

Even after we returned home, I refused to bathe for a month. It didn't matter where or which or whose shower it was—every time I was forced to step inside, I would close my eyes and hold my breath, only for my imagination to kick in and start spinning webs over my head.

In my imagination, I'll always be bathing with spiders.

Clay McLeod Chapman is the creator of the rigorous storytelling session *The Pumpkin Pie Show*. He is the author of *rest area*, a collection of short stories, and *miss corpus*, a novel. Currently, he is writing a trilogy of children's novels titled The Tribe—with book one, *Homeroom Headhunters*, slated to hit the shelves in 2013 from Hyperion. He teaches writing at The Actors Studio MFA Program at Pace University.

River Girl

by GIGI AMATEAU

Look: the solitary midday hunt of a belted kingfisher scouting minnows and tadpoles and salamanders. The summer clothes of girls and boys hugging gray rocks; falling in love. Listen: the lonesome midnight whistle of a coal train moving power and sweat and blood from Virginia's Appalachian Mountains to its capital city. The muffled quack of a mallard drake and his lady snuggling the south bank. The James River is my favorite place: lazy-slow like the duck, fast like the train, loud like the teenagers who got there first, and shrouded like that other king of fishers, the great blue heron.

Layers of history live along this river too. Here on the James, the Powhatan people fished and fought off their enemies. Here, John Smith and Benedict Arnold ventured upstream until rocks and rapids gave them pause. Here on the James, the blacksmith Gabriel, who organized one of America's largest slave rebellions, fled downstream to find help. Here, they dragged him back up to face the gallows. Here, the boatmen navigated hundreds of miles of canal, transporting goods and riches to towns and cities far from port. The river claims all of them as its kin.

I am kin to this river too. Here on the James, as a teen, I laughed and kissed and splashed my way through August. Here I said "Yes!" to the promise of marriage proposed under a pale orange moon one night in July. Here in the James, I taught my child to swim in just one day, when the water was warm like a summer bath and still like a winter sky. Here, I brought my old, dying dog on her last day so she could feel the good breeze once more, lick my hand once more—she, too, a river girl.

This magic river is a city, but only if you make your eye a knowing eye like I did once after running several miles around Belle Isle, the beautiful island in the river. I sat down in the middle of the James on a flat, gray rock as big as two trucks. At first, I saw nothing but water and bedrock, and then I made my eyes look again. Soon, I counted thirty-one great blue herons, frozen still and fishing all around me. Would you believe this magic about the river: Catfish as large as you, weighing one hundred fifty pounds or more, live in the shallow parts with muddy tunnels? Gentle, shy catfish that would hurt no one come out when they see small children.

If only I could bring you with me to my favorite place; if only I could make a living picture and send it from my heart to yours. If I could, I would embed all that I love about the James into your spirit the way the James has worn its path deep into mine, and then the river might endear itself to you too. The river would provide for you as it does me, giving solace in times of suffering, offering such beauty when the eyes are tired, filling up the inspiration well when stories run dry, and providing an obstacle course when the body, mind, or spirit crave challenge. Most of all, you might find in this place an undeniable connection to life—wind, water, earth—and a sense of history such that you would never feel alone again. Ah, but you don't want to reach my place; you want your own favorite place to share with those you love, to leave your mark upon.

I go to my place to find the kingfisher and the coal train and bufflehead and mallard ducks. I go to count thirty-one herons and to search for wise old catfish—they could eat me but they won't. If I look up, I may glimpse the bald-white head of an eagle. With every sighting of this proud bird, I feel astonished that Benjamin Franklin voted instead for the wild turkey as our national symbol. That eagle and I belong to history. We belong with this magic river. On the hardest days—and we all have them—belonging here brings me joy. I am a river girl.

Gigi Amateau is the author of *Come August Come Freedom: The Bellows, The Gallows, and The Black General Gabriel; A Certain Strain of Peculiar; Chancey of the Maury River;* and *Claiming Georgia Tate.* She contributed to the acclaimed anthology *Our White House: Looking In, Looking Out.* Gigi grew up in Mechanicsville, Virginia, and graduated from Virginia Commonwealth University with a degree in urban studies and planning. She lives in the city of Richmond, Virginia, with her husband and daughter.

A Good Lie

by LAUREL SNYDER

Lying is generally a bad idea. Most lies are sneaky and selfish, and some lies are even illegal. Maybe you know this because you've been lied to, and it hurt your feelings. Maybe you know this because your parents have grounded you or yelled at you or confiscated your favorite video game when you've lied in the past. If that is the case, I really hope you learned your lesson! Yes, lying is a terrible idea *most* of the time. However, some lies are gifts. Some lies are made out of kindness. I was once the beneficiary of a very special lie, and it changed my life.

I was eight, and I had a new best friend. We'll call her Lily. Lily was having a slumber party at her house, and because I was her brand-new very best friend, she and I were supposed to share the plaid pullout sofa, while all the other girls slept on the floor around us in their sleeping bags. I felt extremely special.

It was a great party! Because it was almost Halloween, we told ghost stories in the dark, with flashlights. We ate candy and popcorn as we watched a spooky movie. At last, we fell asleep. Then, in the middle of the night I woke up, paralyzed with shame and fear. Horror of horrors—I had wet the bed!

What would you have done in my shoes? At first I simply lay there in the darkness, with my cold pee drying sticky on my legs. I listened to all the other girls snoring and breathing, and worried about what would happen when Lily woke up. Would she stop being my best friend? Would she tease me? Would she have her mom call my mom and send me home right away? Surely all the other girls would laugh. Probably I would never be invited to another slumber party for the rest of my life.

It was awful, lying there, frozen in the bed. But finally my nightgown was soaked all the way through, and I couldn't stand the waiting anymore. I tapped Lily on the shoulder. "Lily?" I whispered in the darkness. "I peed. I peed myself. I'm sorry." I thought I might cry.

Lily just stared at me. "Oh," she said. She was quiet for a minute. She looked like she was thinking things over. I waited, terrified. But that was when Lily told her wonderful lie, the amazing lie that would change my life and make me love Lily until the day I die. "You know what?" she said. "Me too! I peed myself too." Then she smiled.

"What?" I asked. I was so confused. I was certain she had *not* peed in the bed. Her side was dry. I knew it was dry because I'd sort of been trying to creep over onto it, to get out of my own wet spot. "What do you mean?"

Lily nodded her head. "Yes," she insisted. "I did! I peed in the bed too. I'll go get my mom. She'll take care of the mess."

Then Lily got out of bed and walked up the stairs. I followed her, and watched as she woke up her parents and told them we had both peed in the sofa bed. They seemed surprised, but they didn't get mad. Lily's mom found us both clean pajamas, and then came down to the basement with us, to change the sheets.

Some of the other girls woke up, but incredibly, nobody laughed at us. Not even Sandy, the meanest girl in our class. "I peed the bed," said Lily with a laugh. She made a silly face, and everyone laughed along with her. Lily didn't act like peeing in the bed was a big deal, so nobody else acted like it was a big deal. Everyone went back to sleep, and nobody even mentioned it in the morning. We all just ate yummy pancakes and went home with our goodie bags.

Now, I ask you—was Lily's lie a bad thing? A sin? I certainly don't think so. I think it was a gift. It changed me and made me a better person. From that day forward, I tried really hard to be a better friend. I tried to be kinder and more generous. I tried not to laugh at people so much. I tried to grow. Lily had shown a kind of strength I'd never seen before in another kid, and I wanted to be like her. Though I must confess, there was one thing I couldn't fix about myself—sometimes I still peed in my bed. But that was all right because I had Lily, who knew the worst and was willing to be my best friend anyway.

(And still is, to this day!)

Laurel Snyder is the author of many books for kids, including *Bigger than a Bread Box*, *Any Which Wall*, and *Penny Dreadful*. She is pleased to announce that she has not wet the bed in a very long time.

INFORMATIVE ESSAY

Think of something you enjoy doing. Then, in essay form, write the directions
for how to do this activity.

How to Fly

by **WENDY MASS**

The colors become brighter. Your surroundings, sharper. Your heart leaps with the extraordinary nameless wonder of it all. Quickly, before your surroundings fade away, you lift your feet off the ground and fly! The treetops grow smaller as the rings of Saturn grow closer. You can go anywhere you wish. This is your dream, after all. But it is SO MUCH MORE than an ordinary dream. You are having what dream researchers call a lucid dream. You are in a dream, awake.

> **lucid:** [loo-sid] adjective. Mental clarity, clear awareness.
> **dream:** [dreem] noun. A succession of images, thoughts, or emotions passing through the mind during sleep.
> **lucid dream:** The awareness, within a dream, that you are dreaming.

When we are aware that we are in a dream, the entire

experience changes. We are not bound by the dream world, by whatever strange situation our dream self has, well, dreamed up. When awareness floods us, we break free of the bonds of the dream and can control our environment. This is not only hugely entertaining, but it can be life changing. And the best part is, anyone dedicated enough to put in the effort can do it.

The first step to achieving lucidity is to practice recalling your nightly dreams. You'll need a journal, a flashlight, and a pen. When you wake from a dream, don't move from that position. Keep your eyes shut, and run the dream through your mind like a movie. Where did it take place? Who was in it? What were your emotions? Then write down as much as you remember before getting out of bed.

In order to lucid dream, you must become very familiar with the dream landscape. The more you recall, the more you will begin to recognize patterns. Some common dream scenarios are:

- A familiar person appears, but he or she is no longer in your life, or is a celebrity who you are suddenly BFFs with.
- You are in an unusual or unfamiliar place, but you can't say how you got there.
- You try to dial a phone and you can't.
- You are late for school but can't find anything to wear.
- You show up for class on test day and realize you'd never gone to that class before.

- You are invisible. Your cat is speaking to you. One person suddenly morphs into another. Your teeth are suddenly falling out. You are being chased by drooling zombies.

Elements in your dreams that repeat often are called dream signs. Some are universal, and some are unique to each person. After a few weeks of recording your dreams, you will find remembering your dreams gets easier, to the point where you will be able to recall two or three distinct dreams upon awakening. At this point, you should go through your journal and underline all of your dream signs. Once you recognize these, you are ready for the next step—the reality check.

The reality check is just what it sounds like. At specific times throughout your day, every half hour or so, stop what you're doing and ask yourself, "Am I dreaming?" Then do a "reality check" to make sure you are awake. Does the light switch actually turn off the lights? Do the words in a book make sense when you read them? Do you know how you arrived at your current location? In a dream, mechanical objects usually do not work, and printed words are likely to morph into something unintelligible. When one of your particular dream signs appears in real life (For instance, you keep dialing the phone and getting the wrong number.), this is an excellent time to do a reality check.

After only a week or so, do not be surprised to find that the reality checks have begun to enter your dreaming life. You will find yourself in a dream asking, "Am I dreaming?" and you will do one of your reality checks. You will try to read something—but this time the words will change. Or you will try to turn on a light but nothing will happen. Now, instead of a reality check proving that you're awake, it will prove that you're asleep! So you know you're dreaming . . . but then what?

Well, you still have a few hurdles to leap. The moment you realize you are in a dream, you will likely wake yourself up from the excitement of finding yourself in a magical world of your own making, one that actually feels more "real" than reality does. Try to slip back into the dream, but if you can't, congratulate yourself on getting that far and keep practicing your reality checks throughout the day. Then the next time you become lucid in a dream, immediately focus your intent on staying in the dream. Neuroscientists studying lucid dreaming have found that moving around in the dream (spinning, rubbing your hands, stomping your feet) strengthens the lucidity for the dreamer. You can actually see the dream environment becoming solid. You can also verbally announce, "This is my dream and I want to stay lucid!" Your words have power.

Now here is the potentially life-changing part . . .

It helps to have a plan for what you want to do. AND YOU CAN DO ANYTHING IN YOUR LUCID DREAMS. You can soar above your town. You can practice for a big game or an upcoming piano recital. You can stand up to your nightmares, since you see them now for what they are, figments of your imagination. You can embrace someone long gone, and tell them what you never got to say in real life. You can practice for your first date, or paint, or sing, or see what you'd look like with pink hair.

So go out and get your dream journal and start the process tonight! And if at first you don't succeed, well, there's always the next night!

Remember . . .

> "Our truest life is when we are in dreams awake."
> —*Thoreau*

Lucid dreaming will give you a greater appreciation of the amazing powers of the human mind. It will let you soar without leaving the security of your bed. It will show you that the world inside your head is as spectacular as you want to make it.

It will set you free.

Wendy Mass is the *New York Times* bestselling author of twelve novels for young readers, including *The Candymakers*, *11 Birthdays*, *Jeremy Fink and the Meaning of Life*, and *Every Soul a Star*, which features a character who can awaken in his dreams. For more advanced techniques and information about lucid dreaming, try Dr. Stephen LaBerge's books, *Lucid Dreaming* and *Exploring the World of Lucid Dreaming*, and also *The Lucid Dreamer: A Waking Guide for the Traveler Between Worlds* by Malcolm Godwin.

Blueberries

by **MARIE RUTKOSKI**

Throughout my childhood, there was always a large, gold-colored tin in the deep freezer of our garage. The tin was old, dinted, and dented. I would lift its lid, letting the cold exhale onto my skin, and see hundreds of blueberries. They were hard, purple beads lightly furred with ice. I could have plunged my arm in up to the elbow—and I sometimes did. But usually I would scoop out a cup of berries and go sit on the sidewalk to eat them, if the weather was warm. If it wasn't, my mom would make blueberry pancakes that bled purple onto the plate, seeping into the shine of melted butter and the dark gold puddle of maple syrup. We ate blueberries all year. When the tin was empty, we went to Michigan to get more.

My great-aunt Marie's blueberry farm was about three hours from the suburbs of Chicago, where we lived. We went there every summer around harvest time, in late June or July, and slept overnight in the farmhouse attic. The attic was lined with beds on either side: small beds, broad beds, even a bed with mattresses piled high enough to please a princess in a fairy tale.

My sister's favorite was a saggy featherbed my father had slept on as a child. My bed was one I loved for its position, for the way its foot was tucked into the corner where the sloping roof came down toward the floor. I felt cozy in the triangle made between my stretched-out body, the headboard, and the roof.

During the hot, sticky nights, the adults played cards in the kitchen until they were tired enough to sleep. They would sometimes slip outside, always careful where they stepped. In the dark, it was easy to squash a frog.

But this particular memory—of late-night poker and dead frogs—is my mother's, not mine. It has been twenty years since I last saw that farm, and there's a lot I don't remember about it or never knew, like the simple fact that the blueberry bushes were planted so close together that their fruit couldn't be harvested any other way than by hand. I have to ask my parents for such details. When I do, I also have to consider what it means to rely on someone else's memory.

I remember some things. A goose pond and the thorny bramble that grew beside it. The geese themselves. How one bit my younger brother. Three empty doghouses, boards splintered and grayed by weather. The almost bitter smell of the tomato garden. The cool basement with crates for chicken eggs, and mesh racks for blueberries. I remember taking fistfuls of blueberries off bushes and cramming them into my mouth until my tongue was purple, my teeth were a faint blue, and my fingernails were so dyed with juice it looked as if I'd been digging in the dirt.

I remember the last time my family visited. Aunt Marie had

developed Alzheimer's. I was fifteen so I knew what this meant. Her memory was dying. It was leaking away like water from a filled balloon pricked with a tiny hole.

My father got out of the van first. We watched him walk toward her. I heard her voice: angry, suspicious. Frightened.

"Don't you remember me?" my dad asked. "I'm your nephew."

Slowly, she believed him. She hugged him.

We knew it was safe to get out of the van.

We didn't stay the night. It was a day trip, nothing more, though much more time than we had spent on the farm in the previous few years. My father had changed jobs and worked longer hours. He traveled. Family trips to Michigan must have seemed less and less feasible to him until it became clear that there would either be one final visit or none at all.

While he disappeared into the kitchen with Aunt Marie, I went up to the attic to see if it matched my memories. If it really was a place so magical that when my father told me I would never have nightmares if I slept with my feet pointed toward Lake Michigan, I would think of that attic and believe him.

Behind a stack of mattresses, I found a pile of squirming kittens. I brought one downstairs to the kitchen where Aunt Marie and my father sat near a window that overlooked the rows of blueberry bushes. Aunt Marie didn't know there were kittens in the attic, and seemed to have forgotten there was even a cat in the house. "What is the cat's name?" I asked, watching the kitten's mother weave around the table legs.

Aunt Marie hesitated. "Its name is Cat."

I looked at the kitten, its fur damp against my palms. "Can I take this one home?"

"I don't think that's a good idea," my dad said.

"Let her," said Aunt Marie. "She's my namesake. Let her have the kitten."

It wasn't the first time I had heard the word *namesake*. I knew its definition. But this was the first time I realized what it *meant*. Although I had always known I was named after this woman, I had never thought about how she must have felt when she learned which name my parents had chosen for me. I thought about it then. I thought about how soon she would forget me, forget that someone had been named after her, and then she would forget my father, and how she had been like a mother to him for every summer from the time he was five until he was seventeen.

"Okay," my dad said. "Marie can keep the kitten."

"I can?"

"Yes," he said. But the look he gave me was a stern "no."

He was lying. The only reason he had said "yes" was because Aunt Marie would forget the whole conversation. But I wouldn't.

It was unfair. I longed to protest the decision I knew my father had made. There were many things I could have said to him then.

Aunt Marie wants me to have the kitten.

You said I could have it.

And lastly, the accusation that might have worked: *Don't make me be part of your lie.*

I stayed silent. I brought the kitten back up to the attic and left it with the rest of the litter by the dusty mattresses. The attic seemed smaller than I remembered, and I had forgotten about the toilet that stood out in the open. When someone had to use it in the middle of the night, anyone awake would know. I couldn't imagine using it, though I supposed that I had. I couldn't imagine being so exposed.

I sat in the attic, rattled by the conversation in the kitchen and what it had revealed: Aunt Marie could be lied to. This could happen to anyone who forgot. It was frightening, the way not remembering meant that it was easy to believe a lie.

We left the farm. Not long afterward, Aunt Marie was put in a nursing home. She died later that summer.

I am still scared of dying that way. Of not remembering the people I love, or who I am. The act of forgetting is an act of darkness. I fear things getting so black that I can't see.

But lately, when I think about Aunt Marie's blueberry farm, I wonder if there isn't a gentler side of forgetting. A way that its darkness could comfort me, like the low roof above my attic bed did. Not remembering can be a loss. It can leave you open to lies.

But it can also give other people the chance to share memories of their own.

That tin of blueberries in our freezer held exactly twenty-two and a half pounds. I know this because my father told me when I was thirty-five years old. He explained that Aunt Marie had shipped blueberries in cans like that one to pie factories.

"Why did you live there every summer when you were a kid?" I asked him over the phone. I was in my New York City apartment, with my three-year-old playing as we talked.

"I liked it," my father said. A simple answer. But it didn't seem so simple when he paused and said that his parents had had problems. They divorced, remarried. They had fought.

"What do you remember about those summers?" I asked.

He remembered having his ear pressed against the floor-boards as his Uncle Louie listened to boxing matches on the radio while cleaning eggs in the basement. He remembered how at night he and Aunt Marie would sit in the kitchen with the lights off and look out the picture window, watching deer move in the shadows. They could see the stars and the satellites going up into the sky at the same time every night. He remembered how, after a day of harvesting blueberries and mucking out the chicken coop, he would sit with his aunt and uncle in the living room and listen to opera. In August 1968, he watched the moon landing with his aunt and uncle. He was fifteen. That October, Uncle Louie died. My father came for two summers more. After he turned seventeen, he came only for occasional visits. Then he began bringing his children.

"Do you remember how I let you drive the tractor?" he asked me.

"No. How old was I?"

"Oh, about five." He said the seat had been damp with dew. I had howled over my wet bottom.

"And I taught you how to candle eggs."

"Candle eggs?"

"Well, you have to check an egg before you sell it. Make sure there are no flaws—or a chick inside. People used to hold an egg in front of a candle to see through the shell. But we had a coffee can with a light bulb inside. There was a hole in the coffee can lid just big enough so that the bottom of an egg could rest in it. The light would glow through the egg."

I don't remember this. I don't remember what my father tells me—that the farm was bursting at the seams with fruit. Not just blueberries, but also wild blackberries that grew in the thicket by the pond. There were strawberries in the garden. Plums. Peaches. Twenty different kinds of apples. I don't remember that the doghouses were for Cricket, who was part wolf, and Blondie, and canine "guests" that came with friends or farmhands. I don't remember that Uncle Louie built the farmhouse.

But when my father tells me, it is as if we are sitting together in the dark, holding an egg in front of a light, and illuminating something I hadn't seen before.

Marie Rutkoski is the author of seven published, or forthcoming, novels for children and young adults, including *The Cabinet of Wonders*, which has been translated into several languages and short-listed for six state awards. Her most recent novel is *The Shadow Society*. In addition to being a writer, Marie is a professor of English literature at Brooklyn College, where she teaches Renaissance drama, children's literature, and creative writing. She lives in New York City with her husband and two sons.

Banning Books—An Un-American Act

by SARAH DARER LITTMAN

"Congress shall make no law respecting an establishment of religion, or prohibiting the free exercise thereof; or abridging the freedom of speech, or of the press; or the right of the people peaceably to assemble, and to petition the government for a redress of grievances."

—First Amendment, U.S. Constitution

The Founding Fathers understood that the fledgling American democracy would not survive without protecting the free dissemination of ideas. Having seen political and religious dissenters imprisoned and killed for their beliefs under British rule, they wanted to ensure that citizens of the United States were free to criticize the government openly and freely, without punishment.

You might take the First Amendment for granted and assume that these principles from 1791 have nothing to do with your everyday life, but they do—a threat to your basic rights could be happening this very minute, in a classroom or media center near you. Tomorrow your favorite book could be banned.

Every year, hundreds of books are challenged in schools across the country.[10] A "challenge" is an attempt to remove or restrict books or other library materials, based upon the objections of a person or group. If that challenge is successful, it results in a ban; the materials are removed from the classroom or library, and that means no one else has access to them. Banning books is a clear violation of our most basic freedoms, and we should put an end to this all-too-frequent un-American practice.

Over the past ten years, American libraries faced 4,660 challenges based on the material being "sexually explicit," containing "offensive language," being deemed "unsuited to age group" or "anti-family," or containing "violence" and "homosexuality." Others were challenged for their "religious viewpoints."

Parents initiate the overwhelming majority of challenges in schools because they object to their child being exposed to the words or ideas a book contains. Unfortunately, on too many occasions, this is without having actually read the book in question.

Lois Lowry, whose Newbery-winning dystopian novel *The Giver* was one of the ten most challenged books of the 1990s, said in a *Boston Globe* interview: "I just always wish the parents would read the book in full before they challenge it . . . I think

---

10 ALA Office for Intellectual Freedom, www.ala.org/advocacy/banned/frequentlychallenged /challengesbytype.

fiction, in order to say anything, has to startle and upset you at some point. To be a book that affects you, it has to make you think."[11]

Schools are supposed to be places where we encourage young people to do exactly that—to think. It's a place to be exposed to a wide range of ideas and to learn how to evaluate them critically.

One of the most important lessons I've learned in all my years of being a mom is that kids learn most from the behavior modeled by their parents. It makes me wonder what lesson the parents who challenge books are conveying to their kids. That some viewpoints are "acceptable" and "correct" in a democratic society and others are not? That young people don't have the emotional or intellectual intelligence to be able to read about certain behaviors without automatically trying to emulate them?

One mother in Florida went so far as to refuse to return *Gossip Girl* books from the public library after her teenage daughter checked them out because she didn't believe they were suitable for the young adult shelves.[12] She accumulated $85 in library fees before finally returning the books. Then she refused to pay the fees. She was concerned about the behaviors her daughter might read about, but what did her own actions teach her child? That despite the fact that libraries have

11 Louise Kennedy, "Lighting the Way," *The Boston Globe*, May 11, 2003, www.heraldtribune.com/article/20030511/NEWS/305110678.

12 Rachel Jackson, "Mom checks out racy teen books from library and she won't give them back," *Orlando Sentinel*, May 6, 2010, articles.orlandosentinel.com/2010-05-06/news/os-longwood-library-gossip-girl-books20100505_1_library-notes-library-services-manager-library-policy.

established procedures for challenging books, it's acceptable to steal books from the library if you don't like the content? Or that fines are optional?

My parents never restricted my access to books. I read well above my age level, and started reading adult novels way before I probably "should have." But for me, books were a safe way to learn about and process a world that was sometimes frightening and *always* confusing.

While there are many styles of parenting, all parents should be encouraged to be part of their child's reading life. Nothing makes me happier than to hand a book I've read to my kids and hear what they have to say about it. Sharing a book is a great way to start a discussion about the choices characters have made or the situations they've gotten themselves into. And that's another thing I've learned: Being a good parent is all about the conversations.

What parents are not entitled to do, under any circumstances, is to restrict access to the books other kids read.

An important 1982 Supreme Court case, *Board of Education v. Pico*, confirmed this point. While schools might restrict access to books in other ways—such as choosing to not buy them in the first place or not including them in the curriculum—once they are on the library shelves it is a different story.

"The special characteristics of the school library make that environment especially appropriate for the recognition of the First Amendment rights of students," wrote Justice William J. Brennan in his opinion on *Board of Education v. Pico*. "Students must always remain free to inquire, to study and to evaluate, to gain new maturity and understanding." With this ruling, the Supreme Court confirmed that it's unconstitutional to restrict the availability of books in a school library simply because a parent or a Board of Education member or an outside organization disagrees with the ideas or content within.

Books and other materials in a public library have even greater protection because they serve a broader population.

If the Supreme Court ruled on this in 1982, why are so many books still challenged and banned today? This goes back to the First Amendment and "the right of the people to petition the government." *Board of Education v. Pico* pertains only to school libraries and doesn't restrict the right to challenge books—that would be unconstitutional.

In order to fight a challenge, one must have "standing"—in other words, you have to be someone who is directly affected by the ban. Outside organizations cannot come in and do it for you. They can help and provide legal assistance, but first, someone has to be brave enough to stand up and say, "No. Banning books is wrong."

Would you have the courage to do that if someone challenged a book in your school?

The Founding Fathers would be proud of you if you did. As the late Supreme Court Justice William O. Douglas observed: "Restriction of free thought and free speech is the most dangerous of all subversions. It is the one un-American act that could most easily defeat us."

Sarah Darer Littman is the author of *Confessions of a Closet Catholic*; *Purge*; *Life, After*; and *Want to Go Private?* Sarah remains an avid reader of both fiction and nonfiction. She loves cooking, but hates the question: "What's for dinner?" because it means it's time to stop writing. Sarah lives in Connecticut with her family.

GRAPHIC ESSAY / INFORMATIVE ESSAY / PERSONAL ESSAY

If you could change an event in history, which one would you choose and why?

Laika Endings

by **NICK ABADZIS**

LAIKA ENDINGS

Once, not too long ago, I wrote and drew a graphic novel called LAIKA, about a small Russian dog. It was based on a true story – and the ending upset a lot of readers.

Many people still contact me, wondering about that ending, wondering why I told the story the way I did, about how much of it was real and even whether there might be an alternative ending...

Nick Abadzis
www.nickabadzis.com

In 1957, Laika was sent into space aboard Sputnik II. She was the first pioneer of space travel, the first earthling to touch the sky. She died in orbit.

As a kid, I was fascinated by space flight and that's when I first heard Laika's story. The bit about her being sent up by Soviet scientists, never to return – it stuck with me.

That's why, as an adult, I wrote and drew a book about her. Part of the reason was to find some answers as to why that happened to her.

The technicians who built her spacecraft were under huge pressure from their superiors to produce results. They hadn't had time to create a viable system for her safe return to Earth. At that time, in that place, that's just the way things were.

As I researched the book, I found I had a desire to celebrate her life as well as the journey and the Russian engineers that made her the most famous dog in history.

When I was younger, I used to fantasize that maybe aliens had rescued Laika. Maybe she'd lived out her days on the planet Fabuluxxus, lifespan massively extended, faithful companion of Lumino, the Dogstar...

...Or maybe there'd been some miraculous magic doorway through which she'd escaped.

Or maybe someone had just stashed a parachute for her and she'd somehow ejected before reaching orbit.

All those notions are fun and ease the knowledge of her true fate.

Thing is, why should anybody worry about the death of a dog from more than half a century ago? There are animals, and people, all over the planet treated inhumanely every single day, as they have been since Laika flew.

Take your pick of circumstances, wars, and political regimes – the world's still full of unseen and unreported misery. What does the life and death of one dog so long ago mean in the overall scheme of things?

In 2008, the Russian authorities unveiled a memorial statue to Laika, nearly fifty-one years after her flight.

They were rightly proud of their trailblazing cosmodog. She is rendered in bronze upon a rocket shaped like a human hand. Flowers are often placed around the statue.

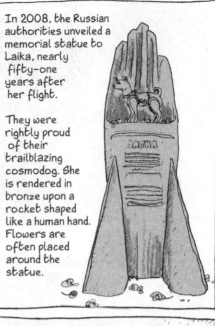

She was the first space traveler. Her journey heralded the dawn of the age we live in – of telecommunications, of smartphones, of the "global community." Everything we take for granted in the modern age began with the flights of the Sputnik satellites.

She may have been an unwitting pioneer, but her journey was heroic.

That's why she matters. She represented and represents us all... just a humble little dog, trained for the mission she flew yet who didn't understand what was happening to her.

The details of why Laika was sent, how she died, and what the world was like then shouldn't be forgotten. And neither should the hope for a new and better age that her flight marked, for all inhabitants of this planet.

We all stand on the shoulders of those who made sacrifices, or were sacrificed whether they agreed to it or not. It's the reason the luckiest of us live freely.

Is there an alternative ending to that?

Nick Abadzis is a cartoonist, writer, and graphic novelist of international renown who has been honored with various awards, including the prestigious Eisner Award for his graphic novel *Laika*. He lives and works in Brooklyn, New York.

LITERARY ESSAY

Look back at one of your written or artistic creations and then describe the
inspiration behind it.

From Seed to Flower

by MICHAEL DAVID LUKAS

Where do fictional characters come from? They aren't born.
They aren't brought by a stork or left in a basket at the author's
doorstep. But they have to come from somewhere, don't they?
According to J. K. Rowling, Harry Potter was based on a boy
who lived down the street from her. Charlotte, the spider in
E. B. White's novel *Charlotte's Web*, was inspired by an actual
spider on a barn on his farm in Maine. And Suzanne Collins,
the author of *The Hunger Games*, says the idea for the book came
to her while watching television. It sounds easy. If you want to
create a fictional character, you just need to spy on your neighbors, hang out with spiders, and watch television. But, trust
me, there's more to it than that. It took me seven years to write
my first novel, *The Oracle of Stamboul*. And creating the main
character, an eight-year-old girl named Eleonora Cohen who
becomes an adviser to the sultan of the Ottoman Empire, was
the hardest part. I can't say what it was like for J. K. Rowling or
E. B. White or Suzanne Collins after their first sparks of

inspiration. In my experience, that first brainwave is only the beginning of the journey; fictional characters start with inspiration, yet they also require deep thought and lots of hard work so that they can develop into real, living, and breathing people.

To me, writing is like taking care of a plant. You start out with a seed and a pot and some soil, and if you water it every day, you just might get a flower. In this metaphor, the seed is inspiration, the idea you have that makes you say, "That would be a cool book." I had two moments of inspiration when I was writing my novel. The first came when I was on a run. I was striding along, listening to my iPod, when I had the idea of a little girl playing backgammon with two old men. I didn't know anything about her except that she was very intelligent and that she played backgammon. I didn't know where she lived or when. And I didn't know anything about her personality. All that came later. My second moment of inspiration came in an antique store in Istanbul, an amazing city (on two continents!) that I visited after spending a year in Tunisia. I was wandering around the store when I noticed a black-and-white picture of a little girl. On the back of the picture was the photographer's name and a date in the 1880s. When I saw the picture, I knew that my main character was a little girl living in Istanbul in the late nineteenth century.

The next step was trying to figure out the basics of Eleonora's personality. (You could say this step is like finding a pot for the seed.) After I had my moments of inspiration, I spent a lot of time thinking about what it would be like to be a very intelligent little girl in Istanbul in the 1800s. I read all the books I could find about old-world Istanbul and very intelligent little girls. I read *Matilda*, *Alice in Wonderland*, and *The Golden Compass*, and I thought a lot about the main characters of those books. I also spent a lot of time thinking about people I know. I thought about the most intelligent people I know. I thought about my little sisters, Anna and Allison, who are both very smart. And I thought about myself. Although I have never been very intelligent and I have never been a little girl, I do know a little something about being human. And in a lot of ways, we human beings are pretty much the same. I know what it's like to be in a strange and wonderful new place. I know what it's like to be lonely. And I know what it's like to be punished for something I didn't do. So I could imagine how Eleonora would feel when these things happened to her.

The next step was sitting down and writing the story. (You could say that this step is like filling the pot with soil.) It might seem backward to write the story before I knew everything about Eleonora, but it worked. A famous writer named F. Scott Fitzgerald once said, "Character is action." What he meant was that we get to know a character best through his or her actions. Think about getting to know a new friend. His mom might say that he's a generous person, but he doesn't share when you forget your lunch at home. He could tell you he doesn't like his sister, but he's always so nice to her when he thinks other people aren't looking. I got to know Eleonora the same way you would get to know a new friend, by watching her in different situations. I put Eleonora into lots of strange spots. I put her in a trunk in the hull of a ship. I put her in the Sultan's palace. And a lot of the time, what she did surprised me, which was fine. A good character, like a good friend, doesn't always do what you say.

Once you have your seed and your pot and your soil, the last step is to water the plant and wait. This step is the hard work of writing, the sometimes boring part, the sitting down every day in front of a blank page even if you don't really feel like it part. This step takes a long time and can be frustrating, but it is probably the most important aspect of creating a character. Imagine if you didn't water a plant; it would shrivel up and die. In the same way, a fictional character needs an author to tend to it, to water it, and to watch it grow. I stuck with Eleonora for seven years because I knew that without me writing, day in and day out, she would wither and die. She would only exist inside my head.

People don't always talk about watering the plant or filling the pot with soil. They like to think that characters are created in a single flash of inspiration. In fact, it's a long process. The inspiration is important, but without the deep thinking and the hard work, all you have is a seed. And who wants a seed when you can have a beautiful, leafy plant or a brightly colored flower?

Michael David Lukas is the author of the bestselling novel *The Oracle of Stamboul*. Michael has been a Fulbright Scholar in Turkey, a night-shift proofreader in Tel Aviv, and a waiter at the

Bread Loaf Writers' Conference in Vermont. He lives in Oakland, California, less than a mile from where he was born. When he's not writing, he teaches creative writing to third and fourth graders at Thornhill Elementary School.

Sex, Drugs, and Rock 'n' Roll

by **LÉNA ROY**

What was it about the black T-shirt displayed high on the wall behind the cash register at my favorite record store that had me so smitten? There were other T-shirts to choose from, but I just had to fall in love with the one that had the words *Sex and Drugs and Rock 'n' Roll* emblazoned in white across the front. I thought that whoever wore that T-shirt must have been the epitome of cool.

Those words strung together. On their own, they were innocuous, but together: BOOM! Cool.

And I had no idea what that really meant.

It was 1981 and the summer I turned thirteen, right before eighth grade. I was brimming with unbridled excitement and energy because I was finally allowed to walk around on my own, exploring the mile distance between where I lived in Chelsea, down to the West Village where I went to elementary school.

This was the summer of the movie *Raiders of the Lost Ark*,

the royal wedding (Charles and Diana), and when MTV made its debut, changing the face of popular culture for good. And I wanted to be the epitome of cool.

It was also the summer my father and I argued about words. Yes, words.

Sex, drugs, and rock 'n' roll.

My father used to quote the opening text of the Old Testament: "In the beginning was the Word, and the Word was with God, and the Word was God."

My father was *the* Father—an Episcopalian priest. He was also a professor and an author, thus language and narrative were important to him.

Episcopalian priests can marry, and my siblings and I were raised by our parents in a seminary, a school where both men and women study to become priests themselves. The church bells would ring morning and evening for services, and there were constant reminders of "God" everywhere. Growing up in this strict environment, I yearned for freedom, for a world without boundaries, for what I thought was a "normal" teenage upbringing.

That summer I was struggling to find my own voice, my own identity. Who was I, besides a preacher's daughter? What words would I use to describe myself?

From the age of ten, I spent all of my allowance and babysitting money on records and music magazines, which provided the lyrics for some popular songs. My money went to Blondie, David Bowie, Elvis Costello, and the Clash. But I listened to whatever was on the radio too, so I wasn't all that discerning. I was hungry for the power of the beats and the music. And of course, the lyrics would float right over my head.

The first argument with my dad that summer was over the lyrics to Foreigner's song "Urgent," which he found in a magazine I had left out in the living room. His irrational rant made him sound out of touch with modern life.

"What junk are you poisoning your mind with?" he railed at me. "Do you know what this song is about?"

I didn't even like the song that much, and didn't understand my father's reaction, so I said, "Who cares? They're only words, Dad."

"They're only words?" My dad's voice echoed around the room in his rage. I had finally done it. I had driven him crazy. "It's about objectifying both men and women!" he said, as he looked over the lyrics.

He grounded me from record and magazine buying so that I could think about his perspective. I felt completely distressed and disrespected. *What a jerk,* I remember thinking.

Legend has it that I cried in my room for a week, trying to think up better words to "Urgent," or at least trying to think about another interpretation of the song's meaning. But even as I stretched my imagination to its limits, I couldn't come up with an alternative message. Maybe my dad was right in that regard, but I didn't want to admit it.

A few weeks later, something astounding and unprecedented happened at the seminary and to my life. Instead of church bells and choral music, we were treated to a new-wave rock concert. The dean of the seminary had an adult son who played in a band called The Clonetones. Somehow they had wrangled permission to give a daytime concert on school grounds. The day was bright, and it was almost surreal as I stood next to my parents, watching, holding my breath. The female singer was the coolest person I had ever seen. She was wearing a white wedding dress and had long bleached-blond hair à la Brigitte Bardot. Cat eye makeup. One of the guys in the band was wearing a sex, drugs, and rock 'n' roll T-shirt.

Their music was powerful, a little dark, and yet their lyrics were clean. I was allowed to purchase their album and talk to the band members. The singer's name was Allison and she was so sweet! I was giddy—I wanted to be her.

I wished that I could walk around in a white wedding dress, combat boots, bleached hair, and heavy eye makeup.

Couldn't that be me? Not while I was still living at home! But if I couldn't go all out, I could at least settle for dying my hair and buying that sex, drugs, and rock 'n' roll T-shirt I coveted, couldn't I?

I remember taking the long walk down to the Village record store with my sister and some friends on a beautiful, sunny day. The black T-shirt with white writing was still there, taunting me.

"Why don't you just put yourself out of your misery and buy it?" a friend said to me. Yeah, why didn't I? I wanted it. I knew that my dad would freak out, but it was babysitting money—it was MY money! Fueled with excitement and self-righteousness, I made my purchase, and I wore it on top of my other clothes.

That was the one and only time I ever wore that T-shirt.

"Hey, look at my new T-shirt!" I announced to my parents, who were sitting in the living room listening to Bach. "Isn't it cool?" (My tactic was to be upfront about it.)

"No, it's not cool," was the response, said in a calm, almost soothing way. "Sex, drugs, and rock 'n' roll. What do you think you are advertising?"

I had no answer except, "I used my own money."

"Oh dear. Then, since you used your own money, I will buy it off you."

I stared at him. Were his words going to trump mine? Was he going to thwart my dreams of being cool? Was he going to impose his own values on my fledgling ones? Of course he was.

"But I used my own money," I repeated lamely.

My dad stood up. "How much was it?" He reached into his pocket.

"Ten dollars." I was sullen, having lost the battle before it even began.

He took out a ten-dollar bill. I pulled off the T-shirt.

"Words matter, Léna. What we say about ourselves matter. The words we use to represent ourselves matter. You know that. We only have so many ways we can express ourselves, and words are the most powerful."

I handed him the T-shirt and stomped upstairs. In my embarrassment and anger, I didn't understand what he was saying.

They're just words. What about the phrase my friends and I used to say to each other: Sticks and stones may break my bones, but words will never hurt me?

But the thing is, I did know better. I knew from the news, from fights with friends, and from arguments with my parents that words had the power to hurt, to cut deeply. I also knew that words had the power to heal. Did I want to tell the world that at thirteen, I was available for sex, drugs, and rock 'n' roll? That I was up for any kind of party?

A few years later, when I was a junior in high school, I asked my father if he still had the shirt, and I couldn't believe it when he said that he did. "I thought that you would have thrown it out!"

"Do you want it back?" he asked me. It was in the bottom drawer of his dresser, and he simply gave it to me. He knew I wouldn't wear it—not because I wouldn't dare, but because I had moved past needing to make that kind of a statement. And he wasn't that strict after all; he had watched me search for my identity through my teens as I morphed from new-wave to goth to 1940s wannabe starlet with my changing hair color, jewelry, and vintage clothing. I may not have had the panache of Allison from The Clonetones, but I had found a way to express myself. And I understood that *sex, drugs, and rock 'n' roll* was not the badge I wanted to define me. Words are powerful, yes, but they can also be limiting.

What then, was I going to do with the shirt? I took it and cut out the words and threw the rest of it away. I had a collage on my wall of meaningful images, from magazines and photographs to quotations and words. And this is where my dad and I came to a mutual understanding—words need context. The words *sex, drugs, and rock 'n' roll* on a thirteen-year-old were either a badge of cool or stupidity, depending on who was looking. Those words on a sixteen-year-old were passé and limiting. However, those same words on my wall next to a picture of my dad became a badge of irony.

Léna Roy holds a BA from Barnard and an MA in drama therapy from New York University. Her first novel for young adults, *Edges*, was published in late 2010. Mentoring has long been the connective tissue in Léna's life—whether through her work with at-risk adolescents in Utah, California, and New York, or through her writing workshops for kids, tweens, and teens with Writopia Lab. Her own artistic discipline was fostered by her late grandmother, author Madeleine L'Engle, who taught Léna to transform the solitary nature of writing into a sacred sense of community where her art and the art of others can flourish.

A Single Story Can Change Many Lives

by CRAIG KIELBURGER

I never thought that a newspaper story would change my life forever. But it happened. A single story taught me that one person can make a world of difference.

It all started one morning when I was twelve, munching on cereal and flipping through my local newspaper looking for the comics.

There on the front page was a story about a young boy in Pakistan. His name was Iqbal Masih. His family was very, very poor. When he was four years old, a man paid Iqbal's parents six hundred rupees, about twelve U.S. dollars, to take him to work in a carpet factory. The man promised to take good care of Iqbal, but he did not keep his promise.

Instead of going to school, Iqbal worked in a cramped, dark, and dusty room for twelve hours a day, six days a week. He ate one small meal per day and was paid one rupee for a day's work—that's the same as two cents.

Most of the children in the factory didn't complain for fear of being punished, or maybe even beaten. Factory guards threatened the children and their families. Iqbal was brave. With the little time he had at home, he told everyone in his small village about the heartless factory owner. But the factory owner was a very powerful man, and the villagers feared him.

Iqbal was forced to work for six years, taking every chance he could to tell others his story.

One day, Iqbal snuck out of work and walked into town, where a group of protestors were marching against child labor. Iqbal told his story to members of a human rights group, and together, they stormed over to the factory and told the owner that Iqbal was never coming back.

Iqbal traveled around the world with the human rights group, speaking out against child labor. His story became so famous that many people stopped buying carpets from Pakistan when they learned that children were working in the factories.

I couldn't believe what happened next. When Iqbal was twelve, he was shot dead while riding his bike. Some people say he was killed by the angry factory owner, but no one ever found out for sure.

Iqbal was twelve. I was twelve.

We were the same age, but our lives were totally different. I grew up in the suburbs with my parents and my big brother, Marc. I played sports and went to school. And I was very much alive.

I was so angry I could hardly breathe. I knew I had to do something. But *what*? I hadn't been looking to make a big difference in the world; I was just looking for *Calvin and Hobbes*! Still, I tore out Iqbal's story and brought it to school.

I asked my teacher if I could talk to my seventh grade class. I was so nervous that my sweaty palms smudged the ink as I clutched the story in my hands. I told my class about Iqbal. I told them about his bravery and how much his story inspired me to speak out for the rights of children. Then I said, "I don't know what, but we have to do something. I need your help. Who will join me?"

Eleven hands went up. That's how Free The Children was born.

We started in my parents' house. We phoned charities asking how we could help stop child labor. But they didn't take us seriously. They just kept asking us where our parents kept the credit cards! I felt really discouraged. *Why couldn't kids help make the world a better place?*

That's when we started fundraising at school instead: washing cars, baking cupcakes, and selling our old toys.

Soon we raised enough money to help build a school for needy kids in India.

It felt great, but there were times I felt like giving up. There were times my parents *really* got fed up with the Free The Children "staff" of teenagers running through the house and racking up phone bills with calls to charities all over the world. I still had all of my regular homework and chores, but now I was running a small organization.

Nothing was easy. As I started to speak out about child labor in schools, the older kids teased me.

"Have you ever met a child laborer?" they'd taunt. I hadn't. So I decided I would travel to Asia on a research trip and meet some.

"Mom, Dad, I really want to take two months off school," I said one September day. I'd just started eighth grade. "I want to go backpacking through Asia. I want to go to Pakistan, India, Bangladesh, Nepal, and Thailand. Oh, and I really want to go by myself."

"No, Craig," my mom replied. "You can't take the subway into the city by yourself. You can't go to Asia by yourself." It was solid mom logic.

I kept asking again and again until my mom banned the word *Asia* in our house.

Finally she agreed to listen to my plan if I could raise at least half of the money for the trip. I was excited, but didn't even have a paper route! My income was zero.

Mom thought she'd heard the end of it. Little did she know, I'd started brainstorming ways to earn money.

I did extra chores around the house and in my neighborhood. Before long, I had saved some money for my trip. And when we got a trusted family friend, Alam, as my guide, I was set to go.

I will never forget the kids I met in Asia. Some picked through trash, others made fireworks in dangerous factories. Their lives were scary. And besides dealing with poverty, danger, sadness, and fear, they'd never been—and would likely never go—to school. They'd never become firefighters or teachers—or anything they wanted to be! They were missing out on childhood. They weren't free.

I knew I'd never feel like giving up again. I made a plan to remember the children I'd met on my trip whenever I felt discouraged, and to remind myself that I had to help them, no matter how difficult the task.

I told everyone about the child laborers in Asia. Then I asked the question, "Who wants to help?" This time, many more hands flew up.

And many more have been raised since.

Back then, we were twelve kids collecting money to help schools. Today, kids in Free The Children school groups all over the world are raising even more money to help build even more schools: 650 schools and classrooms so far, in countries like Haiti, China, and Kenya, for more than 50,000 students worldwide! Last year, 1,300 young volunteers traveled around the world to help build them.

Don't let anyone tell you that one person can't make a difference, or that you're too young. Iqbal's story taught me that one small action can be the beginning of a worldwide movement. So, look around. Maybe pick up a newspaper. Find your story.

Craig Kielburger co-founded Free The Children in 1995 at the age of twelve. Today, Free The Children is an internationally renowned charity and educational partner with the world's largest network of children helping children through education.

Craig has a degree in peace and conflict studies from the University of Toronto and is the youngest-ever graduate of the Kellogg-Schulich Executive MBA Program. He has received the Roosevelt Freedom Medal and the World Children's Prize for the Rights of the Child; he is also one of the youngest recipients of the Order of Canada.

Craig is also a *New York Times* bestselling author who has written nine books. His latest, co-authored with his brother, Marc Kielburger, is *Living Me to We: The Guide for Socially Conscious Canadians.*

Creative Boot Camp

by JOSHUA MOHR

Sometimes we forget to celebrate our imaginations. We take them for granted. We slack and never muster the energy to walk them. We fail to make sure they're eating quality calories. They get lazy and bored.

Neglected, our imaginations lie on the couch, eating Doritos and wearing dirty clothes. Our imaginations spend hours on Facebook stalking our boyfriend's ex-girlfriends or our ex-girlfriend's last boyfriend or our old BFF who we now completely hate or the strange cousin we met at Aunt Martha's crab-feed in July.

We look at our imaginations, sadly curled on the sofa, and we scream at them, "Get up!"

They say, "But *Jersey Shore* is about to start."

We say, "I don't even remember what role you play in my life."

They say, "Shh, Snooki is talking."

Luckily, there's something inside of us, some other force that helps us know that we need our imaginations. There's a part of us that hungers to be creative. I don't know what this force is called, per se, but it's the mysterious drive to write a song or paint a picture or tell a story. I'm not suggesting that we're all going to be professional artists someday. That's far from my point. I'm simply hoping you remember that your imagination is as unique as your fingerprint and that nobody else sees the world the exact way you do. Those songs or pictures or stories you make are wholly individual, wholly you, and more YOU is a beautiful thing to incorporate into your life.

Deep down, even those of us who think we *hate* art know that our lives are better and our imaginations are happier when we allow ourselves the space to be creative. But it's not always easy to carve out time. We're tired from school or worn out with family commitments, friends, sports, whatever. We need a plan, a special health program for our imaginations.

So let's unplug the TV.

Let's snatch the chips away from our reclining imaginations.

Let's whip them into shape. It's time to put them through Creative Boot Camp!

What follows is a how-to guide for making sure our imaginations stay nimble, limber, and inspired, in just three easy steps:

1. **Nutrition:** Food for a bikini-season brain, not the couch slob we talked about earlier . . .

Like our bodies, our imaginations know the difference between quality and empty calories. Make sure you feed it the good stuff. It wants to read books. It wants to paint pictures, write poems, learn how to DJ. It wants to see smart movies.

The old cliché says, "You are what you eat." Let's give our imaginations some of the good sustenance. Fast food is fine every now and then. But a steady diet of junk will leave you craving something of substance, and art might just be the meal that satisfies.

> **2. Regular exercise:** Take a metaphorical jog, do some push-ups. Your imagination needs to be stimulated or it will pull a hammy . . .

Do you want a chiseled, well-defined imagination? Or do you want one that weighs four hundred pounds and is covered in cookie crumbs? It's essential that we get our imagination's heart rate up. But how do we do this? I'm a novelist, so I'll use writing as an example. I write every day. Well, almost. I try to write five days a week. It's my passion. It's what I love doing most with my time. My favorite part of the day is when I get to scribble stories.

Even so, there are stretches when I don't feel like writing. But I do it anyway. It's not just exercise; it's *regular* exercise. Being consistent. Being dedicated. These things create muscle memory. Once art becomes a normal component of your day, if you skip a couple workouts, you'll feel like something is missing. This is a great sign! This means that making art is now a part of your life. But remember to start slowly at first: Can you set aside ten minutes today? What about five? Can you spare a handful of minutes to challenge yourself creatively? You'll be up to speed in no time.

3. **Rest and recovery:** Not to worry, there's enough time to make art and still eat nachos at the mall with your friends . . .

I'm not suggesting that you should lock yourself in a tower and exercise your imagination with every free second. That would be boring and your friends would probably start teasing you, and let's be honest, most pizza places won't deliver to remote artistic towers anyway.

You'll need some rest and recovery, and luckily twenty-four hours is actually a pretty long time. So there's enough space in your day to do everything you want. My suggestion is a bit of balance. Be a writer or musician or painter with some of your day, and also do other things—there's a wonderful world out there, so take a walk, play sports, kiss a boy, kiss a girl, run a marathon, milk a goat, whatever. You can do everything you already enjoy and still incorporate a bit of art into your life. Find the right balance that works for you.

I hope you will follow these three easy steps that will help to bring some creativity into your life. I promise that you'll have more fun with an imagination that's ballet-graceful and football-muscled. Next time you see your good-for-nothing slob of an imagination lying on the couch, burping and channel surfing, just say to it, "It's time to get up and do something."

"Oh, did Mom restock the Doritos supply?" the stubborn imagination might ask.

Be strong. Be firm. Do not be bullied or intimidated. Remember that your imagination secretly wants exercise, whether it admits it or not. It wants to be useful. It wants you to have art, even if it's been a while since the last workout.

"I need you," you say to it pleadingly.

At this, the imagination will sit up a bit, curious and charmed. "You need me?"

"Definitely."

"No more *Jersey Shore*?"

"Let's do something together."

"What should we do?" the imagination asks.

"Whatever we want."

"I'm sort of rusty at this," it says.

"Baby steps," you say. "Come on."

And you two walk off into the distance together, artist and best friend.

Joshua Mohr is the author of three novels, most recently *Damascus*, which the *New York Times* called "Beat-poet cool." He also wrote *Some Things That Meant the World to Me*, one of O magazine's Top 10 Reads of 2009 and a *San Francisco Chronicle* bestseller, as well as *Termite Parade*, an Editors' Choice on the *New York Times* bestseller list. Joshua teaches in the MFA program at the University of San Francisco.

Princess Leia Is an Awesome Role Model

by CECIL CASTELLUCCI

While the predominantly male Star Wars universe is peppered with a few women, there is no question that Princess Leia Organa and her mother, Padmé Amidala, are the most central female characters. However, while Princess Leia is a strong feminist role model, Padmé Amidala reinforces weak stereotypes about women. On the surface Padmé looks powerful, but she makes poor choices and, thus, fails to be a good role model for girls. Leia, on the other hand, is independent, powerful, and pragmatic.

Although Princess Leia and Padmé Amidala both have royal and political power, Padmé Amidala exemplifies the trap seen too many times in stories where heroines lose their agency when they fall in love. In Padmé Amidala's time, while it predates Princess Leia, women are more equally distributed among the upper echelons of power. However, despite the fact that Padmé Amidala is elected queen of her home planet and then senator on a neighboring planet, she somehow becomes distracted by her unhealthy relationship with Anakin Sky-walker. As leader of the rebellion against the Evil Empire, Princess Leia never loses herself, even though she falls in love with Han Solo. She continues to hold her own in rooms full of men and male creatures.

Let us now consider what these galactic ladies wear, and how their choice in apparel further reveals their different approach to femininity and strength. Princess Leia's fashion choices show us that she's pretty practical when it comes to her leading-a-rebellion wear: a white dress that seems to be feminine yet also allows for free movement while running, shooting laser pistols, and swinging across high places on ropes. On Hoth, an ice planet, she dresses for warmth. On Endor, a jungle planet full of green and trees, she chooses a practical camouflage ensemble. One could argue that her Bespin dinner outfit and Slave Leia metal bikini outfit are not utilitarian, but clearly she makes the clothes that other people give her work to her advantage. She even uses her metal bikini as a weapon when she escapes Darth Vader.

Her mother, Padmé Amidala, whose pre-Empire world has many more women in positions of power, seems to fail when it comes to practical fashion choices. While she does have some sensible pants, for the most part, she is burdened by miles of stiff fabric that is impossible to maneuver in; she dons elaborate headdresses and hairstyles and wears a ridiculous amount of makeup. Even her sleepwear seems complicated. Leia, in contrast, likes to keep her hairstyles simple. Her iconic buns keep her long hair neat and out of the way—very important while needing to be ready to run. And yet, she's not afraid to swoop it up, or let it flow. She keeps her face fresh, wearing almost no makeup, and we never once wonder whether or not she is a beautiful woman. Make no mistake, both women have a keen sense of fashion; it's just that for the most part Padmé Amidala chooses clothing that impedes her ability to do her job well.

Skill-wise, I must admit that this mother and daughter are pretty even. They both are extremely smart and capable of formulating and executing plans. They command respect from their peers and are listened to. Leia leads a rebellion, whereas Amidala quietly works from behind the scenes. Both of these qualities are worthy of admiration. The two women are also skilled fighters and show an equal amount of readiness to get into the fight that needs to be done. Both take an active role in saving themselves. While she's Darth Vader's prisoner on the Death Star, Princess Leia stands up to interrogation and docs not give away the location of the rebel base. When Luke Skywalker and Han Solo concoct a half-baked plan to spring her from prison, they may open the door, but she's the one who blasts them out of there by getting them to the garbage shoot. Padmé Amidala, when she, Anakin, and Obi-Wan Kenobi are stuck in an arena fighting monsters, shows her ability to save herself by using a bobby pin to unshackle herself and aid in the fight.

Despite their equally matched skills and ingenuity, when it comes to love, Princess Leia trumps Amidala as a good female role model. In love, they both attract the attention of an independent-minded man, but this is also where they differ greatly. While Leia seems to always maintain her sense of self and is enhanced when she falls in love with Han Solo, Amidala crumbles under the influence of Anakin Skywalker and it destroys her. In the end, Amidala basically dies of a broken heart. It is frustrating and sad to see love make someone as fierce as Amidala less of herself rather than more of herself. Leia and Han run into some love troubles on the planet Endor, but Leia still manages to keep her sense of self, save the day, and not fall apart.

In conclusion, I would have to say that when choosing a role model for girls in the Star Wars films, Princess Leia is the one that I will always follow.

Cecil Castellucci is the two-time MacDowell Colony Fellow, the young adult and children's book editor of the *Los Angeles Review of Books*, and the award-winning author of six books for young adults, including *The Year of the Beasts, Boy Proof, The Plain Janes*, and *Beige*. Her books have been on the following lists: American Library Association's Best Books for Young Adults, Quick Picks for Reluctant Young Adult Readers, ALA's Great Graphic Novels for Teens, Amelia Bloomer, and the New York Public Library's Books for the Teen Age.

The Only Job I've Ever Had

by JOE CRAIG

Some people do physical work to survive. They make a living doing something that requires strength. It might involve digging holes, lifting bricks, or cleaning streets, but whatever it is, it's something that makes them sweat.

Some people don't share that strength, but they have some kind of skill in making or fixing things—useful things, beautiful things, tasty things . . .

Then there are people who don't lift anything, make anything, or fix anything, but they use their brains to help the people who do. They solve the problems, they create the designs, they run the companies.

I don't do any of those things. I write stories. I have grand fantastical ideas that entertain me and somehow, through a process I still find amazing, I'm able to make a living. It's fun and it's wonderful, but it's also a mystery to me how something so unreal can be my sole means of survival.

I've only ever had one job that involved using strength, skill, or the practical bit of my brain and that was in the summer when I was sixteen. It turned out to be a very unusual job. What follows is a true story. The only thing I've changed is the name "Danny Mars."

My parents went away for a few weeks, but I insisted on staying at home to try to make a bit of extra money. I was sick of having to watch the pennies every time I wanted to do anything with my friends. Mom and Dad seemed delighted when I told them. My dad made a living solving problems, by the way—he was a lawyer. So anything that involved me applying myself, whether it was using strength, skill, or practical brainpower, was a great idea to him.

He left me the number of an old business acquaintance named Danny Mars, who he said might give me a job that paid a bit more than a paper route.

The day after my family left, I called the number.

I'd met Danny Mars a couple of times, years before. I knew he was a self-made businessman, but my dad never told me anything specific about his businesses. "Lots of fingers, lots of pies," was all he would say. So I had no idea what to expect.

Someone picked up after two rings.

"Is Danny Mars there, please?" I mumbled.

At first there was no response, but then a man's voice crackled back at me. It was really fuzzy, as if I was speaking to outer Mongolia.

"Dad?" said the voice. "Dad? Is that you?" I could make out the panic in the man's tone. "Is that you, Dad?"

Before I could say anything at all, the person on the other end hung up. The receiver was shaking in my hand. I told myself not to be such an idiot and dialed the number again—but more carefully.

Immediately, the same person picked up. This time he was shouting.

"DAD?!" He sounded terrified. "Answer me! Is it you?"

My throat was suddenly dry. By the time I realized I was holding my breath, the line had gone dead.

Two days later, I was looking for a job in the local paper—without any luck. I had tried to put Danny Mars out of my mind. But then the phone rang.

I picked up right away. The connection was fuzzy like before, but I could make out that the voice was the same. He wasn't panicking this time. Maybe this time I was panicking a little.

"Hello," the man began. His voice was high-pitched and he spoke with a polished accent. "I'm the man who thought you were my father. You phoned a couple of days ago, remember?"

"I remember."

"You wanted Danny Mars."

"That's right. My father . . . Well, I was calling to ask . . . I mean, can I speak to him please?"

There was a long pause, then: "Danny Mars is dead."

I felt a jolt of shock through my body.

"That's a shame," I replied, then immediately felt like an idiot for saying it.

"It is. He's been dead seven years." There was another long pause. Finally the man asked, "So what did you want?"

"Um, I was calling about a summer job." My voice was shaking.

"I see," the man said. "Well why don't you work for me instead?"

My blood started pumping faster.

"Who are you?" I asked.

"I'm Danny Mars's son. I run the business now."

I'd never known that Danny Mars had a son, but I realized it was possible—at least as possible as Danny Mars being dead.

"Can I ask you a question, Mr. Mars?" I said.

"Go ahead."

"When I called you the other day, why did you think I was your father? If Danny Mars is dead, how could I be him?"

"You sounded like him. You do now in fact. The same voice."

So I had the same voice as Danny Mars. I wasn't sure how to feel about that. I tried to hear Danny Mars's voice in my head, but I'd been so much younger the last time I saw him. My voice had changed since then, so nobody would have made the comparison at the time. And now he was dead. I preferred not to think about it.

That was how I ended up going to a warehouse every day that summer to shift crates. I was never told what was in the crates; I just knew how heavy they were and how many I had to stack up or haul across the warehouse. But on my last day I did find out a little bit more about Danny Mars. According to his son, he'd had a rare bone marrow disorder.

"We found a donor," my boss explained to me, "but the donor died in the operation. A perfectly healthy man died trying to keep my father alive."

I looked away and picked a splinter out of my finger. I didn't want to hear the man's family history. I just wanted him to hurry up with counting out my pay.

"Can you imagine that?" he continued, laying bills down one after the other on the crate between us. "A healthy stranger gives his life trying to keep you alive? My father thought he'd murdered that man. Maybe he did. Then my father died."

"I'm sorry." I shrugged, staring at the money.

"So Danny Mars is dead."

"I know."

My boss handed me the money and smiled.

"You deserve this," he announced. "You've worked hard. Thanks for your help."

I couldn't help smiling too. It was more cash than I'd ever held in my life. I was still beaming on the way to the bus stop. And that's when I saw him.

We were the only two people in the street. The light was fading, which gave his skin an orange glow. It was Danny Mars. He was walking toward me, dressed in a long, gray overcoat, staring straight ahead.

I stopped dead. *It can't be him*, I told myself, *you're going crazy.*

"Danny Mars?" I whispered.

The man looked at me. "Yes?" he asked.

I didn't know what to say. In my shock, the only thought

that kept running through my head was, *How can I have the same voice as this old man?*

Eventually, just as he was about to walk on, I gasped, "I work for your son."

Straight away, and as calmly as if I'd asked him the time, Danny Mars announced, "I have no son."

Then he smiled and walked away.

I never went back to the warehouse, and I never told my parents any of this. At first, it was all too unsettling. Then I realized that my dad never asked me about how my summer job had worked out. I thought that was strange. Had he known there was something odd about the Mars family? Had he sent me there deliberately? I decided to make it a kind of test: I wouldn't bring it up; I'd wait for my dad to mention it. He never did.

I still don't know whether Danny Mars is alive or dead, and I still don't know who I was really working for that summer. Over the next couple of years, I spent idle moments making lists of all the things the crates could possibly have contained. Soon the lists grew more elaborate, more fantastical. Those were the first stories I ever wrote. And ever since, I've been surviving not on sweat, skill, or brains, but on what was inside those crates.

Joe Craig is a writer, children's novelist, and musician. He is best known for the Jimmy Coates series. He studied philosophy at Cambridge University and then became a songwriter, winning numerous awards for his compositions before unexpectedly turning to writing books. He is now a full-time author. When he's not writing, he's visiting schools, playing the piano, drawing, inventing snacks, playing cricket and soccer, watching a movie, or reading. He lives in London with his wife Mary-Ann.

Break the Rules

by ELLEN SUSSMAN

Sometimes, when I'm writing an essay, I just gotta break the rules. And I mean BRAKE the rules!

You spelled that wrong.

No, I mean BRAKE. I put my foot on the brakes. NO MORE RULES.

What's up with the caps?

They work. I'm trying to make my point.

And who's talking? Why is this a dialogue? I thought this was supposed to be an essay!

It is. I'm breaaaaaaaaakkkkkkkkking the rules.

Well, then use quotation marks if it's dialogue.

Nah. There aren't really two people talking to each other. I'm kinda talking to myself. No need for all those squigglies.

What's with the gottas, kindas? An essay should be written in proper English.

But I got your attention, right? Sometimes I break the rules to get someone to listen up. And sometimes uptight writerly language creates a distance between the writer and the reader. I'm talking to YOU. You speak my language, right?

Writerly? It's not even a word.

But it's gooooooood. And that matters more than the Rules of Proper Words.

If you break all the rules, then you've got chaos. The reader won't even know what the essay's about.

You know what this essay's about, right? I keep REMIND-ING you, loud and clear. And why would I write an essay about breaking the rules of writing essays without breaking a few rules along the way?

That's a long sentence.

Got your attention, though, didn't I???????

So I break the rules just to get someone's attention? Might as well just drop a stink bomb on the paper.

Won't work. Unless you're writing about stink bombs. I've got another reason for B-R-E-A-K-I-N-G the rules here. I like to think creatively about what I'm writing. Sometimes too many RULES get in the way of creativity. I think: My teacher told me I need an introductory paragraph, so that's what I'm going to write first. HANG ON. Notsofast. Do I really need an introductory paragraph this time? Maybe that works a lot of the time, but each time I write an essay, I want to think about it in a fresh way. What does this essay need? What's the best way for me to explore this topic?

You mean:

Think
Outside
The
Box.

You've got it. Every once in a while there's a teacher or a reader who tries to put the BRAKES on my creativity. NONO-NONONONO, they say. You can't do it THAT way. Well, I see that as a challenge. I've got to convince my teacher or reader: This is great! This is new! This is different and fun and makes me think about the topic in a brand new way!

What if I get an F in English?

F is for *Fear*! *F* is for *Fraidy Cat*! *F* is for *Funless*! Guess what *A* is for?

Absolutely Creative?

Good one! Or: *A* is for: *And You Thought I Had To Do It Your Way??????*

So give me some examples. You know, essays that deserve a little

rule-bending.

My teacher tells me to write an essay about what I did for my summer vacation. BORING. How many times have I written that essay? So this time I draw a beach house. Or I hand in the short story I wrote. Or I write a play about a kid who got kicked out of camp for breaking the rules.

I never got kicked out of camp, but I wish I did, and I can imagine it through writing.

Try it!

My mother would kill me.

Try this one. You're supposed to write an essay comparing two books you read this year. You hate those kinds of essays. Everyone hates those kinds of essays. So you write a story about what happens when the main character of one book meets the main character of the other book . . . like if Romeo met Frankenstein . . . and ALL HELL BREAKS LOOSE.

You can't write hell. The teacher will kill you.

Maybe not. Maybe the teacher's been dying for someone to ShAKe THiNgS UP a little bit.

OK, here's another one. You have to write an essay about a famous person in history who has influenced your life. Whaddaya do?

Well, maybe it's a writer. You SHOW that influence by writing in that writer's style. Maybe it's a politician. You CREATE a political world that your hero would love. Maybe it's an artist. Paint like they do. Or have them critique a painting of yours in an essay, using their voice and artistic style. Picasso gave me some interesting feedback recently.

Cool. I like that one.

We're going to learn a lot of rules over the next years. Every teacher's got a load of them to pile up on your desk. Here's what we do: We learn the rules. Sometimes they really work. I mean, it's good to learn how to communicate well, right? I figure that's what writing is: I've got something to say and I want to share it with you. Once we learn all the rules, we learn one more rule: BE CREATIVE. And creativity might just whisper in your ear: BRAAAAAAKE THE RULES NOW.

Hey, that's kind of a traditional ending for a wacko essay. Can't you come up with something more creative?

Can you? Can you? Can you? Can you? Can you? Can YOU? CAN YOU?

Yes.

Ellen Sussman is the author of the *New York Times* bestselling novel *French Lessons* and *On a Night Like This*. She has also published numerous essays. Ellen has two daughters and lives with her husband in the San Francisco Bay Area.

Acknowledgments

We are grateful to a number of people, without whom this book would not exist. Nancy Mercado (editor extraordinaire) and Lindsay Edgecombe (agent extraordinaire) both provided incredible insight, support, warmth, and answers to our many, many questions. We cannot thank them enough.

It was truly a pleasure and an honor to have worked with each and every one of the authors in this book. They are talented beyond words, and we hope that you all go out and buy their books.

Rebecca: I would like to thank everyone at the Keys School in Palo Alto, California (with extra special thanks to my brilliant and supportive colleagues and the classes of 2012–2015). This incredible community served as my inspiration every single day for six years. Several people—right from the start—believed in this project and believed in me; had it not been for my parents, Nick, Mike, Sloane, Lise, Reed, and Brad, this collection never would have happened. I'd also like to thank my grandmother,

Puggy, my late grandmother, Meme (who I wish was here to read these words), as well as the rest of my family. And finally, to Ellery, the man who loves, supports, and feeds me on the best and the worst days. Without my other half, I could not have made this book whole.

Brad: I would like to thank the amazing English teachers I had growing up at Bullis Purissima Elementary, Egan Junior High, Los Altos High School, and Standford University: Mrs. Rutherford (first and fourth grade), Mrs. Castle (second grade), Mrs. Zierdt (third grade), Mrs. Zierenberg (fifth grade), Mrs. McKinney (sixth grade), Mrs. Bridgman (eighth grade), Ms. Fairchild (ninth grade), Mrs. Baron (tenth grade), and Ardel Thomas (college). These heroes shaped my love of writing, words, and creativity, a love that to this day remains central to everything I am. They sparked something in me that I hope this book provides to others. I would of course also like to thank my parents, Jim and Karen, and my sister, Lauren, for always supporting my strange projects and encouraging self-expression and inquisitiveness. And a big thanks to the roomies of 709 and 1668 for being my home. And to Sara Levin for her insights, love, and editing support. And mostly to Rebecca for being the type of educator who goes way above and beyond . . . both for her kids and for this book. Save the essay!

Index by Essay Type

Index of Essay Prompts

DATE DUE

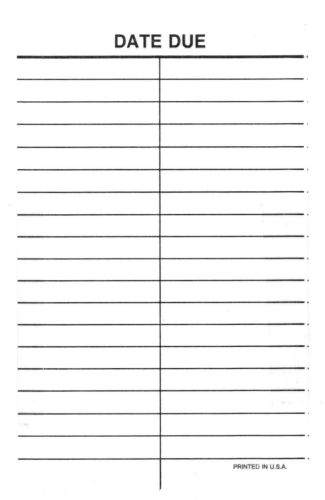

PRINTED IN U.S.A.